About the Author

Blanche Dabney is the author of the bestselling Clan MacGregor books, a series of sweet and clean time travel romances set in medieval Scotland.

Growing up in a small village on the west coast of Scotland, Blanche spent many happy childhood hours exploring ancient castles, all the while inventing tall tales of the people who might once have lived there.

After years of wishing she could travel through time to see how accurate her stories were, she decided to do the next best thing, write books about the past.

Her first romance, Highlander's Voyage, came out in 2018, and reader reaction was positive enough for her to dedicate herself full time to writing more.

Since then, she has published more than half a dozen highland adventures, each filled with the passion, danger, and intrigue that are her hallmarks.

Blanche lives in Haworth, home of the Bronte sisters, with her partner and their two children.

Also by Blanche Dabney

The Clan MacGregor Series

The Key in the Loch
The Key in the Door
The Key to Her Heart
The Key to Her Past

Medieval Highlander Trilogy

Highlander's Voyage
Highlander's Revenge
Highlander's Battle

Highlander's Time Trilogy

Held by the Highlander
Promised to the Highlander
Outlaw Highlander

The Clan MacGregor Series

The Key in the Loch

When a mysterious key sends Rachel Fisher back through time she arrives during a violent time in Scottish history. Her only hope of survival lies with grizzled medieval warrior, Cam MacGregor.

The Key in the Door

To save her life, Jessica Abrahams must convince everyone in the clan she is the missing fiancée of the laird.

The Key to Her Heart

Daisy Stone doesn't believe in love stories. But when she steps into the past she discovers the one man who might be able to give her a happy ending of her own.

The Key to Her Past

Natalie MacCallister lands in medieval Scotland in time to change history for the better.

THE KEY IN THE DOOR

BLANCHE DABNEY

BLANCHE
DABNEY

For Ellen, as ever

Prologue

✤

Morag woke up when her dolly was stolen. She frowned as she sat up. It was the middle of the night. She could tell that by the fact her mother and father were fast asleep in their bed, neither of them moving.

There was no sound outside the window, not even the slightest breeze to shake the shutters.

What had woken her?

She sat up and listened.

What was that noise?

"Psst."

She looked across at the door. It was half open, a hand stretched back inside, a hand that held something important.

"My dolly," Morag said, sliding out of bed. She was too young to be suspicious. She just wanted her dolly back.

She barely felt the cold flagstones under her feet, she was too worried about Mistress Flopsy.

She crossed the floor quickly, pulling the door open in time to see a figure retreating. "Come back," she said, running down the corridor after the shadowy dolly thief.

Back in the bedchamber her parents stirred but then settled once more. By the time they awoke and noticed their daughter was missing it was too late.

Through the darkened corridor, Morag followed the figure, Mistress Flopsy dangling from his hand to taunt and tempt her in equal measure.

"Give her back," she called out as she put on a fresh burst of speed.

"Hush child," the figure replied in a whisper. "If ye wake yon parents ye ken how cross they'll be with ye."

She recognized that voice. She had heard it before. But where? If only he'd show his face.

"Give her back," she hissed, running to catch up with him. "She's mine."

The man turned the corner and vanished from sight.

"I dinnae like this game," she said. "I'm going back to bed."

She was about to turn when she thought about poor Mistress Flopsy, held hostage against her will. It wasn't right. She had to save her dolly. It was her only doll, stitched by her mother and given to her to help her sleep. She couldn't sleep without her.

A door opened at the end of the corridor, the scene lit by a single candle in the sconce on the opposite wall. The figure emerged from the door, his hands empty.

"Where's Mistress Flopsy?" she asked, darting forward, her pudgy hands curling into fists of anger. "Where is she?"

"In there," the man said, pointing through the door. "Why not go get her and then you can both get back to bed like a good little girl? She misses you. She's scared."

Morag didn't even look at him as she passed. She ran straight through the open door and into the darkness. "Where is she?"

She turned back to the door. The last thing she saw was a bare arm stretching toward the handle. The skin was mottled and scarred on the back of his hand, near the wrist.

She remembered that for a long time afterward.

The scar was in the shape of an M for Morag. Or an M for MacGregor. Or maybe an M for malefactor? Had he been branded?

The door closed. A key turned in the lock. The darkness was complete.

Outside in the corridor the Laird was running toward the mysterious figure, a flaming torch in his hand . "Raise the alarm," he said. "Morag's gone missing. Have you seen her?"

"No," the man replied, his voice utterly convincing. "I've nae seen the lass since ah began ma roonds and she was safe in her wee bed then."

"Father," a muffled voice called out from the other side of the door.

"What was that noise?"

"What noise?"

"Unlock this door. Now!"

"It's just a linen closet, ma Laird. There's nothing else in there."

"I dinnae care. Open it. At once, curse you."

"As you wish, ma Laird."

The key went into the lock once more. The door swung open. The Laird stepped inside, holding the torch close to his chest for fear of burning his daughter. "Morag," he called out. "Where are you?"

She wasn't there. There were only shelves of neatly folded cloth. She was gone.

"I heard her," the Laird said, throwing sheets onto the floor. "She's here somewhere. Morag! Where are you?"

More voices began to call out in the keep. A bell rang out in the courtyard. Soon the castle would be swarming with people, all of them calling out Morag's name.

For the moment there was only the Laird standing alone in an empty room, certain that his daughter was mere inches away from him. He could feel her presence and yet the stones could not lie.

She was not there.

She was gone.

Chapter One

Jessica Abrahams was glad of the bills on her desk. It gave her something to look at. She hadn't had a single case for weeks.

Overdue. She set that one down and looked at the next.

Second notice. Third notice. Final demand.

She sighed, tearing that last one open. It was the old familiar wording. Court proceedings, attachment of earnings, must insist, please submit immediate payment.

All she needed was one decent case. One decent easy to solve case and she'd be able to clear all her debts. Shame no one was hiring private investigators anymore. She wondered if it was the summer heat. It was the hottest it had been in years. Was everyone laid in dark rooms, curtains closed, praying for rain?

The only mail she'd had all week had been bills with a couple of thank you notes mingled in here and there.

She leaned back on her chair and looked around the office. Was there anything she could sell to keep her going?

There wasn't much. The computer that had to be crank started, the clock that hadn't worked in months.

What else? There was the desk. Could she sell that? But then how would it look if a potential client walked in and saw her sitting on the swivel chair with the foam bulging out of it in three separate places?

She stood up and walked over to the open window, looking out at the city. Cars crawled along the streets far below, the sunlight reflecting off metal, making her wince at the brightness. There was the slightest breeze but not enough to shift the stifling air inside the office. She ducked back inside.

She added the bills to the tottering pile on the 'to do' tray and then opened the rest of the mail.

Thank you for reuniting me with my lost son. I don't know what I would have done without your help.

She smiled, pinning the card next to the others on the notice board. That case had earned her five thousand, enough to keep her going until a couple of months ago.

The money hadn't lasted forever and she was behind on her rent once again. If things didn't pick up, she was going to have to get rid of the office and start working from home again. She didn't want to do that. It meant nowhere to meet clients.

One decent case was all she needed. She had a grand total of one on the go and it was one she was never going to be able to solve. The case of her next door neighbor.

Footsteps in the corridor, getting louder. A client? Please, God, let it be a client. The footsteps stopped right outside.

She stood up when she heard something fall through the mailbox. Walking out into the corridor she frowned. The mail had already been delivered to her box down in the entrance hall. Had the mailman forgotten something? Who knew she had an old fashioned letterbox in her office door anyway?

She pulled open the door and looked out but there was no one there. On the floor at her feet lay an envelope addressed to her.

She picked it up, hardly daring to hope it might be a case. It was surprisingly heavy. There was something inside. Tearing open the back she reached in and pulled out a small silver key, the end monogrammed with the letter 'M' in swirling intricate metalwork like nothing she'd ever seen. The only other thing inside was a folded piece of cream paper.

Walking back to the office she unfolded the paper. It was a flyer for an open day.

MacGregor Castle celebrates eight hundred years since the building was completed.
Come join us for this historic occasion.
Free entry but donations appreciated for the upkeep of this historic property. Sunday, August 22nd 10am to 5pm.
Refreshments and souvenirs will be available for purchase.

In amongst the text were ink drawings of the castle itself. It looked a pretty enough place. She paused, frowning as she looked at the drawings again. A memory sparked inside her. She knew that castle. But where from?

She put the flyer down on the desk and examined the key again. No explanation, no letter to go with it. Just the flyer. Addressed to her in hand-writing she didn't recognize. It was a mystery.

She smiled. Maybe it was a case after all. The open day was in two days time. She did a mental calculation of the amount of fuel in her car. Would it make it to MacGregor Castle? Where was it anyway?

She booted up the computer and made a coffee while she waited for it to load. It wheezed into life just in time for her to stir in the sugar and then she was finally able to connect to the internet.

She'd learned long ago she had to act as if she didn't care if the computer loaded or not. If she sat in front of it, nothing happened. It would obsti-nately slow down to glacial speeds while she cursed it and all its kind.

Then one day she happened to be boiling the kettle while it loaded and she turned back to find it ready to go. Since then, she'd worked it out. If she acted like she didn't care whether it loaded or not, it would be ready to go as fast as lightning. Need it for something urgently and it refused to play ball.

Sometimes she even said out loud, "I don't even need the computer for this." Then she could be sure it would be ready and willing to work like an over eager puppy.

She sipped at her coffee while she looked up the castle. It was in the Highlands of Scotland, not too far from the Isle of Skye. Why had she been sent the flyer? What was waiting for her there? Why the key? What secret might it unlock? So many questions and no answers came to mind.

She looked into the history of MacGregor castle. One of the medieval fortresses of the Highlands, it had stood for centuries as the Clan MacGregor went from strength to strength, moving from the initial wooden buildings to a stone behemoth that dwarfed the surrounding countryside.

It had fallen into ruin in the early thirteenth century. From what she could work out the Laird and Lady at the time had retreated into their chambers when their daughter went missing. They left their steward in charge and he managed to ruin the clan and the castle within twenty years, throwing money around that they didn't have.

The daughter was never found, just one more mystery never to be solved. She smiled as she imagined being a private eye back then. She'd have gladly taken on that case.

It seemed such a shame that a castle that had been looked after for generations could be ruined in less than one. The place had remained in ruins for centuries after that before some Victorian Laird had begun restoration work, turning the place into a country seat.

All of that was very interesting but didn't explain why she'd been sent the key and the flyer. Still, she was a fan of history, and of Scotland. A little vacation wouldn't do her any harm. It would mean she wouldn't see any more bills arriving for a while.

She decided to write the day off. Unplugging the computer, she pocketed the key and the flyer before heading out of the office. Locking it behind her, she had the strangest feeling that she wouldn't go back in there ever again. She shook the feeling away. It was nonsense.

She took the stairs rather than the elevator, stepping out into heat that almost knocked her backward. At once she felt sweat forming on her back. She crossed the street and stopped at the convenience store on the corner.

Digging in her handbag, she found a couple of coins of indeterminate age. It was enough to get a loaf of bread and two cold cans of cola.

"Going home early?" Barry asked when she put her items down on the counter.

"Not much happening at the minute," she replied. "How are you?"

"Still hoping you'll solve the case of the lonely store owner."

"I told you, Barry. You're not my type."

"What's wrong with me?"

"You're married with three kids."

"Oh yeah, I forgot about that."

She smiled as she left, the ritual completed once again. She wondered what she'd do if someone actually did want to marry her. The thought was enough to make her laugh. She had zero money, zero prospects, and sometimes suffered from night terrors. That and the ugly scar on her arm made her quite a catch.

It took half an hour for her to get to her apartment building. She thought about getting a cab but doubted they would take an IOU as payment. The thought of getting on the tube in this heat made her feel ill so she walked, finding herself thinking about MacGregor castle again.

She would have to try and find out more before she went north. How did a child just go missing like that? Why did they lock themselves away rather than look for her? Did they have other children? What happened to them if they did? And did they know their steward was running the clan down into ruin?

Maybe the visit would give her some answers. The people working at the castle might be able to answer them for her.

She climbed the steps to her building and pushed open the door. Inside was quiet, the noise of traffic dying away as the door swung shut behind her.

The elevator was out of order again so she climbed the stairs, feeling the need for a cold shower growing. Sweat was pouring down her.

She stepped out on the third floor, not surprised to find Caroline sitting cross legged in front of her door, her eyes far too old for her ten years. "Locked out again?" she asked.

Caroline shook her head. "They're arguing."

"Quelle surprise." She held a can out.

Caroline took it gladly, opening it and draining half the contents in one go. "How old are you?" she asked as she wiped the open can across her forehead.

"Thirty-one. Why?"

"Maybe when I'm thirty-one, I can be like you. Have my own place. Then I wouldn't have to listen to shouting all day."

"Yeah but you'd have bills to pay too."

"I could get a job. I could work for you, like your apprentice or something."

"I think the child labor laws would have something to say about me hiring a ten year old."

"Next year?"

"Maybe." She sank to the floor, opening the loaf of bread and tearing a hunk off, passing it to Caroline who devoured it so fast she thought the kid might choke. "It does get easier, you know? It won't always be like this."

"What if it doesn't?"

She shrugged. "I'll have to keep feeding you then, won't I?"

Caroline looked up at her, blinking rapidly. "Could you be my mom?"

"What?"

"You don't shout at me. You make sure I've got things to eat. They just yell at each other and then go out drinking. Please, let me move in with you. I'll be good, I promise. I'll wash up and clean for you and everything."

"Listen, Caroline, it's not quite that simple."

"Why not?"

Jessica took a sip from her can, wondering how she'd gotten herself into this. How was she supposed to explain to a child that yes, her parents were the worst, but when she'd tried to report them to social services, they didn't want to know?

"I can't just take you away from your parents like that. There are rules we have to follow."

"Why?"

"Why what?"

"Why do we have to follow the rules?"

"We just do."

"Caroline!" A man's voice roaring down the corridor. The girl got to her feet, handing the empty can to Jessica.

"See you later."

What killed Jessica was the look of resignation on the kid's face. It made her want to run after her, sweep her into her arms, take her into her apartment, get her dress clean, feed her properly, at least run a brush through her hair.

Who was she kidding? She could barely look after herself, let alone another person. She might as well wish for the moon as to be able to help Caroline. She'd already done all she could, reporting the family three times to social services. Each time it was thank you for telling us and we'll look into it.

Then nothing. Sooner or later the kid might end

up dead and then she'd spend the rest of her life blaming herself for it.

But what else could she do? Run away with her? The police would find her quick enough and that would be career over, hello jail.

She emptied her pockets onto the kitchen table before walking through to her bedroom, lying back and closing her eyes, wondering how her life had come to this. An apartment with rent in arrears, a job that no longer paid, no skills beyond being good at reading people, no qualifications, no future. She couldn't even save a ten year old from misery.

She would have cried but it would have done no good. The heat made her forehead burn. A headache was coming and there wasn't going to be anything she could do about it. The curtains blew in the breeze, then fell still. The only sound was the rumble of traffic on the street far below.

The next thing she knew she was asleep. She knew she was asleep because it was dark. She was surrounded by darkness. She was hammering on a door, banging her fists against the wood, yelling for it to be opened.

Then she heard something. A woman's voice singing a lullaby. In a strong Scottish accent.

"I left my babby lying here,
Lying here, lying here.
I left my babby lying here.
Tae go and gather blaeberries."

S he woke up with a start. What was that? Her mind felt foggy from the heat and the impromptu nap. Someone was singing nearby. Was the sound carrying from one of the other apartments? No, it was closer than that. She got up and walked to the door as the voice grew louder.

"I found the wee brown otter's track,
Otter's track, otter's track.
I found the wee brown otter's track.
But ne'er a trace o' my baby, O!"

S he crossed to the spyhole and looked out into the corridor. No one was out there. The sound was behind her. There was no radio in there but the voice was definitely coming from the kitchen.

She walked in and there was only the key sitting on top of the folded flyer. Had she folded it? She must have done.

The key seemed to glow with a white light. Without knowing why, she picked it up and put it to her ear. The voice was already dying away but she could still hear the lovely gentle woman singing softly just for her.

"I found the track of the swan on the lake,
Swan on the lake, swan on the lake.
I found the track of the swan on the lake,
But not the track of baby, O."

T hen the voice was gone. She looked at the key and then shook her head. She was going mad. It had to be the heat. That and worrying about Caroline. And the gnawing stress and anxiety of knowing she was on the verge of losing her apartment. No wonder she thought she was hearing things.

It was all in her head. There hadn't been a voice. Nonetheless, as she walked back through to the bedroom, she took the key with her.

She lay down with it under her pillow and tried to remember the lullaby. Already the memory was fading. She'd heard it before somewhere. But where?

She closed her eyes once more, hearing a fading woman's voice in her head as she drifted off to sleep.

"I found the trail of the mountain mist,
Mountain mist, mountain mist.
I found the trail of the mountain mist,
But ne'er a trace of my baby, O!"

Chapter Two

E ddard MacGregor sat on the end of the jetty, looking out across the water at the mainland. So close and yet so out of reach. Would he ever set foot on it again?

He had just replaced two of the rotten boards with fresh wood and was taking a moment to himself, a rare occurrence. There was always someone needing something done.

He walked back and forth along the jetty a few times, making sure the boards were sound. Finally satisfied he stepped onto the grass and headed back to the village, his hammer in his belt, the few spare nails gripped in his hand. On an island so small iron nails were a valuable commodity.

The walk to the village didn't take long. He strode through the heather as if it weren't there, marching quickly, breathing in the sweet air of the island.

When he reached the village he heard a curse from inside the tavern. Pushing open the door he found John wrestling with the barrels, trying to lift one off his foot.

"Let me help with that," Eddard said, lifting the barrel into his arms and heaving it up into the air. "I told you not to play skittles with them. You're too old."

"I struggle for quarter of an hour to lift that into place and you walk in here and hoist it in the air like it's a newborn lamb. The devil take you, Eddard."

"If you dinnae want my help, I can leave you to it." He went to drop the barrel, catching it again at the last second.

"Nae, lad. I'm only joshing with you. Get it up there and join me in a taste test?"

"I havenae time to drink. I need to get on."

The door to the tavern opened and an elderly face peered in.

"Early for a drink, isn't it?" Eddard asked. "Are you coming in?"

"Ah've been looking for thee, Eddard. Have ye time to see to ma roof?"

"All the time in the world for my neighbor. Take care of that foot, John. Call me if it swells."

"I will."

Eddard followed Michael outside, slowing his pace to match the older man as they made their way across the village green, the sheep barely looking up at them as they passed.

Two minutes later Eddard was sitting atop of Michael's house, pulling out wisps of rotten thatch and tossing them to the ground. He looked around at the other houses. All of them were falling apart.

The Laird wouldn't let things fall to ruin if he knew. It was all the fault of that cursed steward of his. He only cared for what he could get from the clan, not what he could give to them. "It'll all need replacing next year," he called down. "I'll do what I can for now."

"I cannae afford the reeds," Michael called back. "Ronald has doubled the taxes on them twice this season."

"You grow them. Why not just use them fresh cut and dried?"

"He'll find out. He always does."

"Och, the man's not got eyes everywhere." He

paused to wipe the sweat from his brow, looking out at the loch. In the distance a boat was approaching. Two figures were inside and the boat was sitting low in the water. "Knights," he said, climbing back down from the roof.

"I told you he'd find out," Michael said, looking nervously across the green as if he'd be able to see the water through the houses. "He heard us talking about it."

Eddard shook his head. "He doesnae ken everything."

"Then why are they coming?"

"I dinnae ken but no doubt we'll find out soon enough."

"What if they've come for you?"

"I doubt it. I think he likes the idea of me being in exile. It would spoil his fun to have me executed."

Michael tapped him on the shoulder. "It was meant tae be, lad. You wouldnae have come here if you hadnae been exiled and look what you've done for us since you came. God sent you, Eddard MacGregor."

"And I suppose God made me kill Ronald's brother?"

"You didnae mean it. How could you have known he'd tipped his own sword?"

The conversation stopped abruptly as a bell rang out. The knights were getting close. Shutters slammed across the green, villagers running inside, barring their doors. It wasn't a good idea to be in the open when Ronald's men came on patrol.

By the time the two knights reached the village only Eddard was still out in the open. The two knights sneered at him but said nothing, marching past and kicking open the door to William's house.

Eddard strode over in time to see them dragging William out, his wife trying to hold onto his arm, screaming at them to stop.

One of the knights let go long enough to slap poor Brenda across the face, sending her sprawling into the dirt.

William went mad trying to reach his wife. The knights both reached for their sword but they never got a chance to use them. Eddard was behind them.

He reached out, grabbing their heads in his enormous fists, slamming them together, their helmets making a mighty crash as the two men staggered backward, turning to see Eddard smiling at them, his arms folded.

"You're a long way from MacGregor Castle," he said. "You should be more civil."

One of the knights took a step forward, the

other one waiting, hand on sword hilt. "We're taking a malefactor to pay for his crimes. You will make way for the clan guard or you'll pay the price."

"William a criminal? And what crime has that man commited, pray tell?"

"Milling his own grain."

"Maybe if your man hadn't tripled the tithe at the castle mill, he wouldn't have had to mill his own."

"That's not for you to argue. The law is plain. All grain is to be milled at the Laird's mill."

"I dinnae hear the Laird himself complaining."

"The steward speaks for the Laird as you ken. Now stand aside. We are taking him with us."

"No," Eddard said, stepping between them and William who was still comforting his stricken wife. "I dinnae think you are."

"You would stop us? You without so much as a sword or shield."

"Dinnae need them."

The knights looked at each other and then pulled out their weapons. Eddard didn't move. He waited perfectly still for them both. They lunged at the same time and that was their first mistake.

Both got in each other's way, bumping together

and giving him time to lean to the left, avoiding the tips of the sword. As the knights realized what he'd done he turned, grabbing the nearest by the waist and lifting him into the air.

With a grunt he hurled him into his companion, sending the two of them rolling into the dirt together as they roared in pain.

He walked over, snatching the swords from their hands before they knew what was happening, tossing the weapons away behind him. "Get yourself back to the castle where you belong. We are a free people on this island and you'd do well to remember that."

"You will pay for this," the nearest knight spat, helping his companion to his feet. "We'll be back for you."

"You ken where I live. I'll be waiting. Tell you what, why not send Ronald? I'd be glad to have a word with him."

The knights limped away, not looking back.

"Is she all right?" Eddard asked William. "The baby okay?"

Brenda was sitting on the stump outside the house, hands cradling her huge bump. Her eyes were closed.

"She'll be right enough," William said. "I thank

thee, Eddard. I dinnae ken what I would have done without you here."

"You'd be strung up at the castle," Brenda said, her eyes opening. "And I'd be a widow. Help me inside."

Eddard watched them go. Once the door was closed, he picked up the two swords and examined them. Poor quality work. He bent one of the blades with no effort. The second had an impurity in the metal. One solid blow and it would shatter. The money was clearly running out over at the castle. Either that or Ronald wasn't bothering to check the work of his blacksmiths. Neither were good signs.

If only the Laird and Lady would emerge from their own exile, the exile so much worse than his own.

He had been banished to Kirren Island more than a decade earlier for killing the steward's brother.

He hadn't even wanted to fight. Alexander had badgered him again and again but he would never fight someone so weak. Then Alexander had gotten his attention by beating Eddard's sister. She never recovered.

He had to fight then but he didn't intend to kill Alexander. He only had to close his eyes to remember it like it was yesterday. Flicking the sword out of his opponent's hand and then catching it, nicking him on the cheek with the tip to prove he could have killed him.

Alexander falling to the ground, foaming at the mouth seconds later. The word poison spreading across the crowd.

The trial was perfunctory. Ronald, steward to the Laird and Lady, saw one chance to get rid of Eddard and took it. If he'd thought he could get away with executing him, he would have done. Ronald dared not risk it. The people would have revolted at the idea, Eddard was the most popular lad in the castle. Nonetheless, he was found guilty of poisoning the steward's brother, exiled to Kirren Island, there to remain for the rest of his life.

What was that exile though compared to that of Cam and Rachel? He knew what happened to his sister, killed at the hand of Alexander. He could only guess at their pain, their daughter missing, never seen again. Alive or dead? No one knew. Their torture would last a lifetime and perhaps into the eternity beyond.

Their pain could be the only reason why they'd listened to the steward. He told them their only remaining child would be safe at the abbey. Why would any couple in their right mind let their son out of their sight after what happened to their daughter?

Something about this didn't add up.

He shrugged. He'd probably never understand.

All he wanted was to get back to the castle where he belonged. He spent years trying to think of a way to achieve that, a way to get the steward thrown out, get things back to the way they should be, stop the clan self-destructing under Ronald's cruel grip.

The only way he could think of was to find little Morag, though if she were still alive she wouldn't be so little anymore. She'd be in her early thirties. How would they even know she was their daughter?

What he needed was someone he could use to convince them Morag had returned. Who it was didn't matter. What mattered was getting the Laird and Lady to come out of their chambers and govern the clan once more, throw out Ronald before he ruined them all.

A small figure came running across the green toward him. "Eddard," the boy said. "Come, quickly."

"What now?" Eddard asked, wondering if he'd get a moment to breathe.

"A ghost. At the old abbey."

"A ghost? Someone's playing a trick on you, little Thomas."

"They're not. I saw it myself, just now."

"Right, hold on. Tell me this tale from the beginning."

"I was getting some stone to help father with the back wall. The best stone's in the cloister, you ken?"

"I dinnae need to ken about the stone, Thomas. Tell me about this ghost."

"Well, I looked up and there was nothing there, then I heard a door opening and then there was a woman up there. I saw her through the window of the church. She came out of nowhere."

"But what makes you say she's a ghost?"

"Because she's up where there's no stairs. There's no way up or down to that window. She has to be a ghost. See for yourself."

He grabbed Eddard's hand, pulling him to the edge of the village, pointing all the while at the abbey. "Look, over there, do you see her?"

Eddard squinted. He could see something over there. A figure was pacing back and forth on the other side of the window frame. "That's no ghost," Eddard said. "That's a woman of flesh and blood."

"It's a ghost, I tell thee. It has to be. How else could she just appear like that?"

"I dinnae ken but the easiest way to solve a mystery like this is to go have a look."

"Not likely. I'm not going back over there. It's haunted."

"Suit yourself."

Eddard walked across the open toward the abbey, looking at the window the whole way. The abbey itself had long since crumbled. Plans had been made to rebuild but that was before little Morag had gone missing. The new abbey had been built over on the far side of the island. This place was little more than a crumbling ruin.

The old abbey had a look of utter desolation about it. The tower had long since collapsed, the roof gone. Only a few walls remained, that of the west side of the church being the tallest. It contained four windows without glass or shutters. Below them a long drop on either side to the rock strewn ground.

Back when the abbey was first built a walkway ran along that level to a spiral staircase at the end. The stone from the staircase was long gone but the walkway remained. It was there that the figure stood, looking out at Eddard as he drew nearer.

He squinted again, seeing her face in more detail. He knew that face. He'd seen it somewhere before. But where? He quickened his pace. The only way to get an answer to his question was to ask her. As he looked up again, she slipped from view, a scream reaching him from behind the wall.

She was falling. It was at least twenty feet to the ground from there. If he didn't do something she'd be dead before he had chance to ask her a single thing.

He broke into a sprint, praying he would get there before it was too late.

Chapter Three

✧❧✧

Jessica woke up after her dream with something stuck to the side of her face. She lifted her head slowly, reaching for her cheek at the same time. Had she fallen asleep halfway through a candy bar?

She'd done that before in a hotel and the results had looked like a dirty protest against the cleaning standard of the First Class Inn, which ironically was a surprisingly clean establishment.

It wasn't candy. No brown smears on the pillow. She peeled the object from her face. It was a key. Why did she have a key stuck to her face?

The memory came back to her a second later. It was the key she'd been sent in the mail the previous day. The flyer was on the floor beside the bed, no doubt blown through by the gusts of wind that had woken her in the first place.

Getting out of bed, she slid the window closed, paused a second, then locked it. She might as well prepare for the road trip to Scotland.

There wasn't much point getting breakfast. She knew for a fact that all she had in the kitchen was a six month old half box of crackers she was sharing with the mice, and a bottle of milk in the fridge she dared not touch, in case it moved again.

She had visions of opening the door and finding it emerging from the bottle like something out of Little Shop of Horrors. Her plan was to hire an exorcist and hazmat removal team at some point when she had enough cash in hand. Until then, the fridge was like her lovelife, better not to think about it.

She dug her one suitcase out from under the bed, ignoring the dust bunnies that tried to come with it. With the case open and ready, she turned to her closet, picking something that would be suitable for August in Scotland. Snowsuit? Parka?

It couldn't be that cold, even in Scotland. Eventually, she settled on a couple of pairs of black pants, her cleanest shirts, red check for that lumberjack vibe. On top of them she added underwear for two nights, just in case. Then a pair of boots followed by sunhat and shades, no harm in being optimistic, right?

She thought about bringing suntan lotion but decided against it. That would be tempting fate. She left the case open and went through to the bathroom, finding herself humming as she packed her wash bag.

"I left my babby lying here, lying here, lying here." She stopped, wondering where she knew that song from.

Catching a glimpse of herself looking confused in the mirror, she grabbed a hairbrush and began to belt out Aretha Franklin, collapsing into laughter as she managed to misspell R-E-S-P-E-C-T twice in quick succession.

She knew she should be more miserable about the fact she was rapidly running out of cash and had no cases coming in but she found herself surprisingly optimistic as she brushed her teeth before packing the brush into the bag.

A road trip was still a road trip and she hadn't been to Scotland before. It was just one of those places that was eternally on her to do list, a bit like learning French and doing Ryan Reynolds. She'd tick off that list eventually.

This was a start. If Ryan Reynolds happened to be shacked up in Glasgow teaching French while she passed through? Well, that would be a bonus.

With the case closed and waiting by the door she scanned the apartment a last time. Windows locked. Curtains closed. Bed made. Dishes done. She even left the light on in the bedroom so it would look like someone was home while she was gone.

Not that it mattered. If a burglar happened to break in, he'd be more likely to leave something for her out of pity than take any of her paltry possessions.

She pushed the case on its wobbly wheels as it reluctantly slid out into the corridor. She turned to lock the door and when she turned back Caroline was standing at the corner near her apartment, as if she'd been waiting for her.

"You okay?" Jessica asked.

She wasn't. She looked like she'd been crying again. "I'm okay." Caroline nodded toward the suitcase, sniffing loudly as she did so. "You going somewhere?"

The sound of yelling came from the apartment around the corner.

"Just for tonight."

"Can I come with you?"

"You don't even know where I'm going."

"I don't care. It's got to be better than here."

"I can't take you with me. I'm sorry."

"Why not?"

Jessica let go of the suitcase, holding her arms out, wrapping them around Caroline and holding her close for a moment. "When I get back, I promise I'll do something about them."

Caroline pulled away, wiping her nose with the back of her hand. "It won't make any difference. They won't listen. Please, let me come with you."

"I'll be back before you know it. I'll bring you some ice cream with me, okay?"

"Promise?"

"Promise."

They shook pinky fingers before Caroline stepped aside to let Jessica pass.

Outside, she looked up at the building. "Poor kid," she thought out loud, making a mental note to ring Social Services again when she got back. Would she be able to adopt her?

The rational adult inside her knew it was a non-starter but the optimist whispered that maybe, just maybe she could be her mom.

She walked to where her car was parked, pulled

the flyer out from under the wiper and looked at it. MacGregor Castle Open Day. "I get it," she said, looking up at the sky. "I'm going, all right?"

With the suitcase safely stowed in the trunk beside her tent and sleeping bag, she climbed into the car, holding her breath while turning the key in the ignition. It started on the third attempt. "Make it, Reg," she said as she revved the accelerator. "You can do it."

The car spat fumes, hitched, and then roared into life. "I never doubted you," she said, patting the wheel. The fuel gauge wobbled up to around the halfway mark. That wasn't enough to get her there.

She would have to use her emergency tenner, the one hidden at the back of the glovebox behind the antacid pills and the few cassettes that still worked in the music player.

She wedged her cellphone into the holder, loading Google Maps before typing in MacGregor Castle.

Five hours thirty minutes. She'd be there by half past one if she didn't stop.

She did stop. Once for fuel, kissing goodbye to the emergency ten pounds and feeling oddly sorry to see it go. The second and third times were to cool down the engine which was enjoying the sunshine as much as a vampire with a migraine. All it wanted was a little cold spot in the dark.

She felt much the same. The only way to keep it from overheating was to keep the heater blasting. She then had to counter that by having the windows open so the noise of the motorway made her ears ring as she slowly made her way north.

She crossed the border just after eleven, letting out a quiet cheer. The invaders of the past would have had to fight for every inch and yet she was able to simply drive across with only a single "Welcome to Scotland," sign to mark the momentous occasion.

The further north she traveled the more hills appeared. Gradually the hills became mountain ranges, the car cutting between them along bending ribbons of road. Lochs would appear momentarily behind trees. She would get flashes of azure blue before they vanished behind thick foliage once again.

It was when she stopped for the last time to let the engine cool that she was able to take a proper look around her.

She was standing on the edge of a quiet country road. There hadn't been another car since she turned off the motorway. It looked like wherever MacGregor Castle was it was out of the way.

All she could see was brown and gray mountainsides, the tops wreathed in fog. In the valley below her a river ran, gleaming in the sunshine. The air felt fresher than any she'd ever known and she breathed in great lungfuls of it.

Oh, to live up here all the time. She imagined a little cottage down there by the river. Just her and Caroline and a Scottish Ryan Reynolds, bearded, kilt on permanent standby, ax in hand, forever chopping wood for her to watch. The thought made her smile. If she was dreaming why not dream big?

Make it a hunky medieval warrior fresh from slaughtering baddies and saving orphans, come to ravish her by a roaring log fire before singing her to sleep with some simple Highland ditty. On the breeze she seemed to hear the lullaby again. "I found the trail of the mountain mist."

Her thoughts went back to the key. It was as if it had already unlocked things in her mind, things she hadn't known were there. A desire to get out of the city, to live somewhere peaceful, at least for a little while.

The desire for a family too. That had been thoroughly hidden away at the back of her mind. To have a family you needed a man. To get a man you needed something desirable about you. She had zip, nada, a great big zero.

"All I've got is you, Reg," she said, turning to look at the car which responded by ticking over quietly. She turned away from the view reluctantly, starting the engine on the second attempt and then continuing on her way.

The roads grew narrower still, branches encroaching the verges, leaves slapping her wing mirrors, potholes starting to appear.

After ten minutes in which the road surface continued to crumble and the trees grew even closer, she was about to stop and write a strongly worded letter of complaint to the Google Maps route guidance team, certain she was heading down a dead end straight into a cabin out of a horror movie.

The only ax-wielder down a road like this would definitely not be a Highland hunk. Her fuel guage was dangerously low once more and if she kept going much longer she wouldn't have a choice about going back to the main roads, she'd be stuck in the middle of nowhere with a long walk to a gas station.

"Right, I'm turning around," she said as the

suspension bottomed out in the deepest pothole yet. Just as she said it the trees fell away and she was out in the open, three quarters of the way up a mountain side. Up on the peak the mist had cleared - *I found the trail of the mountain mist* - and there was the castle, looking just like it did in the flyer.

The sight took her breath away. It was half Disney, half Dracula, all turrets and crows with ivy growing up the sides. If a princess had emerged at a window to sing to the birds she wouldn't have been surprised.

There was a small parking lot to the left hand side of the drawbridge and she turned into it, amazed the car had made it. The engine groaned when she turned it off. Whether it would start again remained to be seen.

Hers was the only car there and when she got out and approached the drawbridge there was no sign of anyone. In fact, there were no signs at all. No opening times, no *toilets this way*, not even a *gift shop doesn't take cards* or *don't litter*.

If it wasn't for her car she might have thought she'd gone back in time. The only noise was her feet crunching on the gravel and the crows cawing high up in the sky.

She stopped at the drawbridge for a moment.

She had two choices. See if they'd let her in early or camp up and wait for tomorrow. Camping with no food in the car wasn't that appealing even with the view of the mountain ranges to enjoy.

Her stomach was already rumbling with hunger. She had to see if the place would let her in, if only to eat something. She had about three coins left in the whole world. Hopefully it would be enough.

She crossed the drawbridge and stopped in front of the huge oak iron studded doors. She pushed. Neither of them opened. Above her, she could see the murder holes directly above her head and she felt glad she hadn't traveled back in time. It would be a formidable task to try and take a castle this grand.

An idea occurred to her when she saw the keyhole in the door. Returning to the car, she retrieved the silver key and tried it in the keyhole. It didn't even turn. "Not for that door then," she said out loud, pocketing it and trying to work out what to do next.

"What would the mailman do with parcels?" she asked. "They have to go somewhere."

She almost laughed when she realized. There was a door to her left that was open. She'd spent so long looking at the grand entrance that she hadn't even noticed the modern door hidden in the shadows of the tunnel that led to the huge main gate.

She stepped inside, calling out, "Hello," as she went. After the bright sunshine the gloom of the interior made it hard to see a thing. Something moved ahead of her and she looked up at it as a voice spoke in a strong Scottish accent.

"We're closed. Come back tomorrow."

Chapter Four

✿❀✿

The figure came into focus. It was a woman in her late seventies, her hair a shock of white that made her look like a ghost. It was only when she switched on the desk lamp beside her that Jessica was certain she wasn't dealing with a spirit of the castle.

"Did you nae hear me?" the woman asked. "We're closed. You're breaking and entering."

"The door was open."

"Aye, to let the air in. That doesnae mean any Tom, Dick, or Sassenach can come waltzing in here like she's the Laird's wifey. Get thee gone before I call the police."

Jessica held a hand up. "Listen, just give me a

minute. I'm not here to steal from you. There's no need to call the police."

The woman's hand was already on the phone. "I'll dae it. Watch me."

"Someone sent me this," Jessica said, reaching into her pocket and bringing out the key. "Any idea what it is?"

"What's that?" the woman asked, her expression changing to shock before the scowl returned. "No one here sent you that. Now, what is it you be wanting?"

"I just wanted to have a look around the castle."

The door beside the old woman swung open and an elderly man in a black suit appeared.

"What are you grumbling at now, Sandy?" he asked. "Hello, who's this?" His hand stretched out toward Jessica. "Name's James MacGregor. How do you do?"

"Jessica Abrahams," she replied, taking his offered hand.

He shook firmly, not gripping her too tightly before letting go. "What can I do for you, Miss Abrahams?"

"Jessica."

"Jessica as you wish. How can I help?"

"I was hoping to have a look around the castle."

"I told her," the woman snapped. "Not open until tomorrow."

"Och, it's not like we've got much tae do," he said with a smile. "Forgive my wife, she's always crabby before the open days. Lots to prepare. Look, I can give you a guided tour if you like. Gets me out of doing any proper work."

"James MacGregor, you're meant to be out pruning them rose bushes."

"They've lasted two hundred years. I'm sure they'll wait an hour. Come this way, lass."

He walked back through the door, beckoning for Jessica to follow. She went after him, trying to ignore the death ray coming from his wife's eyes.

Once she was through the door she found herself in a narrow corridor that came out in the courtyard of the castle. Behind her were the still closed main doors.

On all sides walls loomed upward, towers in each of the four corners of the castle. Narrow windows remained like arrow slits in some places but in others they had been replaced with stained mullioned glass in a variety of colors.

The courtyard was cobbled, trestle tables set up in a horseshoe shape around the edges. "Ready for the stalls," he said. "We've got our own wine to sell, honey too. Now, what would you like to see?"

"I'm not sure. What is there?"

"Well, what do you ken about the clan?"

"Not much."

"You must ken something. People dinnae just turn up here out of nowhere."

"I do."

"Aye, I can see that. Do you ken anything at all about the MacGregors?"

"I know that the castle fell into ruins for a long time after the Laird and Lady's daughter went missing."

"'Twas an awfa' case, that one. Eight hundred years ago and still pains us MacGregors. They never found her, do you ken that?"

"What do you think happened to her?"

"I dinnae ken but I can show you where she went missing if you like."

"I'd like that very much."

"This way."

He crossed the courtyard to a set of external stairs that climbed seemingly into the wall. The rooms inside seemed to appear from nowhere. "The castle's a bit of a maze," he said by way of explanation. "A lot of collapse and rebuild and collapse again. The back end sticks out over the moat but most of the oldest rooms are in this bit. Up here."

They went up a spiral staircase and came out into a narrow stone corridor, the floor bare flagstones. It smelled ancient and the flickering bare bulbs above their heads gave out little more light than candles would have done. The windows here were all boarded up.

"We dinnae use this part much," James said by way of explanation. "To be honest, the place is far too big for two old folks but that's just the way it is."

"Why not move somewhere smaller?"

"Because we're guardians of the place for the next generation. Despite her grump, Sandy feels the same as me. It's in our bones, this place. We could never leave it." He stopped by a door and turned the handle. "Here you are."

Jessica peered inside. It was an empty cupboard, no more than five feet square.

"Can you guess what it was used for?" he asked.

"Linen closet?"

The man's eyebrows shot up. "Extraordinary. How did you guess that?"

"I must have read it somewhere." She couldn't tell him the truth, that she'd somehow known it was a linen closet. As he'd turned the handle she'd already pictured the inside, shelf after shelf of neatly folded cloth.

"The story goes," James said, pulling the door shut again, "that the Laird heard her in here and came looking but when he opened the door, nothing. She was never seen again."

"What do you think happened?"

"I think there are things in the Highlands that no one will ever be able to explain. I sit on the battlements sometimes at night and I swear I can hear the old guards talking to each other. One time I heard some lass sing a lullaby to her bairn when there was naeone in the place but me. No doubt that all sounds daft to you."

"Not at all," she replied.

"This way. This is the Laird's chamber coming up, where Morag was last seen before she vanished." He stopped outside another door. "Blast," he said, rattling the handle. "Locked." He pulled a ring of keys from his pocket and began running his fingers through them. "It should be here somewhere. Can you see a silver one with an M on it anywhere? Where is the blasted thing?"

"James!" Sandy shouted from down in the courtyard. "There's a man on the telephone for you."

"Be right down," he shouted back before turning to Jessica. "It'll be the papers. They want tae come up and snap a few things on the open day. Bide me a wee while?"

"Of course. Take your time."

He headed back down the corridor and she listened while his footsteps slowly faded away. Turning back to the door, she tried the handle herself. It rattled in place but the door didn't open.

She pressed her ear to the door. Someone was singing on the other side, the noise faint. "I left my babby lying here." The singing dissolved into tears which faded away into nothing, leaving Jessica hearing only her own breathing.

Almost without realizing she was doing it, she brought the key out of her pocket. "It's not going to fit," she said out loud. "Of course it's not going to fit. I'm imagining it, that's all."

She slid the key into the door and tried to turn it. She realized she hadn't breathed only when her lungs began to burn for air. Gasping, she took a breath, looking down at her hand which was trembling. The key was turning slowly in place.

She pulled the key out and looked at it for a moment before pushing the door open. So the key worked? So what? That didn't mean anything.

So why did the air suddenly feel charged with electricity? And why had she heard someone on the other side?

She stepped through the door and realized at once that her guide had got things wrong. She wasn't in a bedroom. She was on the battlement walkway that ran around the four sides of the courtyard.

She looked back through the door and stopped dead. It wasn't the corridor. It was a room lit by flaming torches. She was still trying to work out what was going on when hands fell on her from behind. "Hey," she said, twisting in place and shocked to find two men in medieval armor grabbing hold of her. "Let me go."

"She looks like Rachel," one of them said. "Is that nae strange?"

"Ah thought it was her."

"Let me go!"

The other knight replied to his colleague, ignoring her efforts to free herself. "You dinnae think it's Morag come back, dae you?"

"Not our job to think. Let's take her to Ronald."

She fought again to get free from their grip but her kicks only hurt her feet, crashing into the solid metal covering their calves. They were much stronger than her, a foot taller, their faces hidden behind the visors of their helmets.

She dug her heels into the ground but still found herself being dragged backward along the battlements toward the far tower. "Help," she called out, her voice muffled by a hand over her face before she could say anything else.

The two men pulled her through a door and then into a tiny stone room. They shoved her to the floor, withdrawing and pulling the door closed before she could get back to her feet.

"Quite the security team they've got," she said out loud as the door was locked and she was left alone. There was only one small window above head height, lighting the space just enough for her to tell it was empty .

Empty except for a single wooden stool that looked like it might collapse if she sat on it. She tried banging on the door but it did no good. She shouted herself hoarse but that achieved nothing either.

She tried consoling herself with the idea of suing the security firm the castle had hired. Unlawful arrest, kidnapping, wrongful imprisonment. They'd be in a lot of trouble when they finally let her out.

If they let her out.

She refused to think about that option. It was too crazy. She tried her key in the door but it didn't fit. They had to let her out. It would be crazy of them not to.

Any less crazy than a corridor turning into a room and knights in armor grabbing hold of you?

She had no idea how long passed before the door opened again but by the time it did her fear had turned to anxiety and then to boredom mixed with fear.

She wasn't sure what to feel when the key turned once more and she was surprised to see an overweight man in a beautiful medieval costume entering. He wore expensive looking green hose on his legs, above that a tunic with gold thread sewn into it in swirling patterns that looked much like waves on the ocean.

A thick fur hung from his shoulders and he held it close around his neck with his gloved hand as he entered. "Cold in here," he said, shivering slightly. His face looked pale, gaunt almost despite his bulk.

"I hadn't noticed," she replied, trying to push past him.

He shook his head. "My men are right outside. You would be wise to remain compliant."

"Compliant? Your men locked me in here for no good reason and if I don't walk out of here in the next minute, you're going to be looking at one heck of a lawsuit."

The man ignored her, grabbing her chin in two fat fingers, squinting as he looked at her. "You look too much like her for comfort. If you had red hair instead of blonde, you'd be the spitting image of Rachel. How did you get here?"

"By car, how do you think?"

"What is a car?"

"Seriously? I know you're reenacting or something but can you step out of character and see how much trouble you're in?"

"Very well," he said. "I will give you one chance. We can do things the simple way or the difficult way. How did you sneak into my castle?"

"I didn't sneak in. The MacGregors let me in."

"Which MacGregor? I shall have the man before me to speak the truth so no lies."

"James and Sandy."

"There is no James MacGregor here."

"Go and see for yourself. He's on the phone right now."

"What's a phone?"

She again tried to push past him. "I've had enough of this. Out of my way."

He grabbed hold of her, the smell of him up close making her nostrils wrinkle. "How did you get on the battlements? The door was locked."

"I used a key."

"What key?"

"This one, all right?" She brought the silver key out of her pocket and waved it in front of him.

"Interesting," he said, stepping out of the room and beckoning for her to follow. "If you're telling the truth, that key will fit the door, correct?"

"Of course."

"Then this way."

He walked along the battlement, her following, the guards behind her. The group stopped by the door to the corridor inside. "Pass it here," the man said, grabbing the key from her hand before she could protest. "Let's see if you're telling the truth."

He pushed the key into the door and unlocked it, pushing it open. She found herself staggering back at the sight before her. Instead of a room or a corridor she saw the ruins of an abbey through the doorway.

Behind it the shoreline and the deep waters of a loch. They were high up above the ground.

"Through you go," the man said while she was still reeling in shock.

When she didn't move, the guards shoved her through the door. She scrambled for balance, right on the edge of a narrow walkway at least twenty feet above the ground. By the time she righted herself the door was closed and locked.

She slammed her fists against it, hoping this was all a dream. The pain in her hands felt real enough but this couldn't be happening. Doors went into rooms. The rooms didn't change each time you unlocked them.

She could hear nothing through the door. Beside it was a window and she peered out, seeing that the door led to nowhere. Whatever room had been on the other side of the wall was long gone, presumably into the pile of rubble and rafters far below her.

She began to pace back and forth along the walkway, trying to stay away from the edge. How could she get down? The wall looked sheer and the ground was too far for her to jump. She leaned through the window again, looking for answers on the other side. There was no help there.

Where was she? It was a ruined abbey of some kind. Was she hallucinating? Had she banged her head on the castle's low ceilings and passed out? Or had the car crashed on the way up to Scotland and this was some kind of coma dream? Would she know if it was?

The abbey was on an island surrounded by water. The mainland surrounded it, mountainous and desolate looking. There was no one to be seen.

No, that wasn't true. There was someone walking across the grass in the distance, heading her way. She leaned further out to look closer. The stone was weak and began to crumble, falling away from her.

She lost her balance trying to right herself, her heels catching the edge of the walkway and sliding into the empty air.

With a scream she found herself falling, her hands catching the stone and gripping onto it for dear life. "Help!" she cried, her fingers coming loose.

Any second and she'd fall. If she survived she'd break more than a few bones if she couldn't hold on.

"Help!" she cried again, her grip failing her. She tried to pull herself up but her arms weren't strong enough. Stone began to crash to the earth around her, sending up plumes of dust that make her cough and splutter until she felt a sneeze building up in her nose.

She tried to hold it in but it came out none-theless, making her head bang against the wall, the shock enough to loosen her fingers from their precarious hold on the walkway.

Then she fell.

Chapter Five

Eddard felt alive for the first time in years. When had he last run like this? His heart pounded and his lungs burned as he leaped over the top of a pile of rubble, sliding along the biggest of the stones and then half tumbling, half running down the other side.

Twisting his body, he barely slowed as he turned the corner and then she was in view. He put on a fresh burst of speed. She was about to fall. He sprinted the last few feet along the base of the wall.

She was no ghost. She was wearing the oddest clothes but she was real and she was about to lose her grip, her feet scrabbling at the wall, desperately trying to get a purchase.

He skidded to a halt underneath her, looking up

as she fell with a scream. He braced himself. He saw her falling through the air, her hair wild, her arms flailing. Time stood still for the briefest of moments and she was just hanging there.

Then he blinked and in the time that took she'd landed in his arms with a thud. He fell back with her on top of him, her face inches from his own, staring into his eyes in a mixture of fear and relief.

"Are you all right?" he asked.

She blinked, saying nothing, as if she wasn't sure she was alive. He couldn't help noticing the sparkle in her eyes, ocean blue and glittering like they were reflecting the sun out at sea. There was depth there, depth like nothing he'd ever seen before. Pain too. Why was she in pain?

"Are you hurt? Can you nae speak?"

"I'm fine," she snapped, untangling herself from his body, getting slowly to her feet. "I thought I was dead. Am I dead?"

"It was close enough. The reaper came to visit but he didnae stay. What fool errand sent you climbing up there? Do you nac ken how dangerous it is."

"I didn't climb up there."

"Flew up then, did you?"

"Look, I just need to get back up okay. Can you give me a hand?"

There was a creak above them and then a screech of stone against stone. The ground shook violently.

Eddard grabbed her hand, pulling her back as she began clambering up the rough stones at the base of the wall, oblivious to the danger. "Get away from there," he said. "Cannae ye see it's collapsing?"

"I have to get back through that door before it's too late."

Another creak and then a long line zigzagged through the masonry like lightning down a tree trunk. At any moment the whole thing would come down. "Away from it," he said, yanking her backward.

She tried to fight him, still not heeding the danger, trying once again to climb the wall despite it already collapsing around her, giant stones crashing to the earth, sending up plumes of dust into the air.

His patience running out, he picked her up and threw her over his shoulder, dodging more falling stones as he carried her toward the safety of the empty church.

As he crossed the threshold there was an enormous crash behind him and he looked back in time to see the rest of the wall gone. There was only dust and his ringing ears to tell him it ever stood there.

"Put me down!" She kicked and hit but he ignored her, keeping his arm around her hips until he was sure the danger was gone.

"You're one foolish woman," he said, loosening his grip at last. He barely let go before she was on the floor, sprinting back toward the collapsed wall.

"Where is it?" she asked, disappearing into the dust cloud before emerging again a second later, coughing and spluttering. "Where's it gone?"

"Where's what gone? Are you mad, woman? Come away from there."

"The door. I need to get through the door."

"There's nae door nae more, just kindling and rubble."

"No, there must be. I have to get home."

"What are you blethering about?"

She grabbed his tunic, staring wildly into his eyes and he was again taken by how blue they looked. He frowned. She looked like someone he knew. Who was it?

"The key," she suddenly said, her eyes widening as she grabbed his baldric. "It's the key that did it.

He stole it from me. I have to get it back. I have to get home. I can't stay here. I don't even know where here is."

He gently pulled her hands away, holding them in his own. "Take a deep breath, lass. You're nae making any sense. Who stole your key? Have we a thief here on the island? Name the blaggard."

"You don't understand. I have to get it back."

"Right, haud on. Let's start at the beginning. What key is this you're talking about?"

She sighed, sitting heavily on the nearest rock, putting her head in her hands. When she looked up, he was again struck by the fact he knew that face. Where did he know that face from?

"I was sent a key in the mail. When I used it at MacGregor castle, something happened, I don't know what. I went through a door and ended up with these guards who locked me up. It was some kind of portal, like in the movies. Oh God, let this be a dream."

"It's nae dream. You're as real as I am. What about this key of yours?"

"This guy appeared and he took the key off me and then he shoved me through onto that ledge where you saw me."

"But that door up there doesnae go anywhere. It

used to lead into the dormitory but that fell many years ago. How could you come through it?"

She looked up at him, blinking as the dust slowly settled around them. "You're not listening. The door was like some kind of magic door or something. I know it was the key. I need to get it back so I can unlock the door back at the castle. That will send me home."

"And where is home?"

"You'd never believe me."

"Try me."

"No. Listen, where's MacGregor Castle?"

"About thirty miles that way," he said, pointing past her.

"Then that's where I'm going. I have to get my key back."

"Haud on a wee moment. You think you can just walk in there? Get in without the steward's men approving it at the door? If you could just saunter inside I'd have moved home years ago."

"They'll let me in. They have to."

"The only woman they'd let in without question would be the princess come back from the dead."

"What?"

"Never mind." A thought. That was where he knew her face from. An idea began to form.

"Then what the heck am I supposed to do?"

She looked just like the Laird's wife. Rachel. It had been a long time since he'd seen the Laird and Lady and that was what had thrown him. If she looked so much like the Lady then could she possibly be…?

"Is your name Morag by any chance?"

"Not you as well. No, my name's not Morag."

"What did you mean by that? Not you as well?"

"You're the second person to think I'm this Morag. Who is she?"

"The Laird and Lady's missing daughter. You're a spitting image for the Lady, you could be her child."

"But she went missing when she was a little girl. I've just been reading about that." All of a sudden her face turned ghostly white. "Hang on. Are you telling me you think I'm Morag? The girl who went missing in the thirteenth century?"

"It is the thirteenth century."

"Oh God, I had a horrible feeling you would say something like that. What year do you think it is?"

"Twelve - oh - eight, praise the Lord."

"Twelve - oh - eight. Oh is right. Oh indeed.

Oh heck, what is going on? I must be dreaming, that's it. This has to be a dream."

"You almost died a minute ago. That wasnae any dream."

She managed a wan smile. "You would say that if this is a dream. Well, if this is a dream, I should probably just go with it until I wake up. How do you propose I get into MacGregor Castle?"

Eddard didn't answer at first. He was listening to something. Suddenly he grabbed her and yanked her backward. A second later the rock she was sitting on was covered in fresh rubble from the top of the pile. "How did you know?" she asked, looking down at his hand holding hers. "That it was about to fall, I mean."

"I heard it shifting. Did you nae hear it?" He let go of her.

She shook her head. "Thank you, for saving me. Twice, I mean. I guess I could be a bit more grateful."

He shrugged. "I cannae get over how much you look like Morag." He grinned, the idea fully formed. "You need to get the key that's in the castle, right?"

"Yes."

"You get the key and use it to open your magic door and go home?"

"Exactly."

"So we convince them you're Morag. It willnae be hard. They let you inside. Then you can get the key, the steward gets booted out on his arse and I go back home."

"Convince them I'm Morag? How will that help me?"

"You dinnae understand. The Laird and Lady have been hiding away ever since she went missing, letting that villain run the clan intae the ground. Make them believe you're her and they'll come out of hiding and see the damage he's done. I swear once they ken the truth, they'll throw him out and you can search the entire place to your heart's content."

"But I'm not their daughter."

"You could be. If we teach you a bit of an accent, and a couple of other things."

"Like what?"

"I dinnae ken. I didnae ken her that well. What we need to do first is go to the new abbey, convince the abbot you're her. Do that and he'll lend us his boat to get over to the mainland. We have to take his. If the steward's guards see any other boat on the water they sink it with the weight of arrows brought to bear. We just have to make the abbot believe you're her."

"But where am I supposed to have been all these years?"

"I dinnae ken. Come back from memory loss or pilgrimage or kidnapping or something. We'll think it up on the way."

He was already walking but she grabbed his arm. "Stop, wait a minute. I'm not Morag. I don't know anything about her. He'll know we're lying and then what?"

"Haud on, I have an idea. Angela knew the lassie when she was wee. She'll give us a clue."

He began walking again, leaving her to jog to catch up to him. For the first time in a long time, he allowed a little bit of hope into his heart.

He'd grown used to life on the island, accepting that he would never get to see the inside of his home again.

But maybe, just maybe, that was no longer going to be the case.

If he could just get the Laird and Lady to come out of their own exile, maybe he could end his. It all rested on convincing them she was Morag.

One little lie for so much good, it had to be

worth it on the Scales of Heaven. The clan could be saved before it disintegrated, the steward would be the one living alone and scraping a living. It was almost too good to dream it was possible.

The walk to Angela's little cottage down by the shore took an hour. They went past the new abbey, following the rabbit trail that ran around the edge of its walls. His companion looked up at the wall as they went by, saying nothing. What was she thinking?

He looked at her, marvelling at just how much she looked like the Lady. She was different though, her hair wilder, not held neatly within the confines of a barbette.

"What's your name?" he asked as they walked.

"Jessica. Jessica Abrahams."

"Nae," he replied. "It's Morag MacGregor. Understand?"

"But it's not. I told you-"

"From now on you are Morag MacGregor and nothing else. Get used to the name, be ready to respond to it whenever anyone says it."

"Morag. Got it. And you? What's your name."

"Eddard MacGregor."

"So we're related?"

"Do I look like royalty? We're the same clan,

that's all. Dinnae expect birthday gifts from me. You're no my kin."

"Not even a card wishing me happy returns?"

He didn't answer. A moody silence descended.

Eddard wasn't sure what to make of her. She was clearly out of her mind. All this talk about keys and magic doors made no sense to him.

That didn't matter. What mattered was she was the key to his return. He could use her to get back into the clan and get revenge on Ronald for everything he'd done. He might even get to take his place as steward.

No, that was too much to hope for. He would be grateful just to be back in the castle where he belonged. He would miss the island but it had never been his home, not really.

His home lay within the soaring walls of the castle he knew like the back of his hand, even if it had been more than a decade since he'd been there.

Angela's cottage came into view, standing alone like a lighthouse on the clifftop. He thought about how many times he'd sat fishing with her on the beach below. She had been like a mother to him ever since he'd arrived on the island, talking softly to him, bringing him out of the dark and smoldering fury he'd felt when he was first exiled.

Angela was outside chopping wood. From this distance she might be mistaken for a young woman even though she was pushing seventy.

She stood perfectly straight, tossing logs into the barrow from the pile she'd made. She waved when she saw him, turning to vanish inside. He knew what was happening. The kettle would be hooked over the fire, ready for their arrival.

"Is she a friend of yours?" Jessica asked. "Angela, I mean?"

"She's a friend to all," he replied. "Even you with your mad hair and mad clothes and even madder ways."

"Hey, what's wrong with me? I'm friendly enough, aren't I?"

"I fear you're insane."

"Don't hold that against me. I'm still a nice person."

"Who tries to climb collapsing walls and talks about magic keys to doors that dinnae go anywhere?"

They'd reached the house by that point, the smell of flowers soon swamped by the smoke that emanated through the thatch topping the cottage.

The door was open and Eddard ducked as far as he could, still scraping his head on the arch before getting inside. He stood up straight again in time to see Angela place three steaming pewter mugs on her tiny trestle table.

"Come in," she said. "I see you've brought some company today. Who might you be, lass?"

"Jessica Abrahams."

Eddard shot her a look. "You're supposed to say Morag."

"She does look like Morag would," Angela said. "The perfect mirror of Rachel, God save them both. Come and sit down, get some tea inside you. You look like you need it. 'Tis a cold enough day."

Jessica took one of the mugs from the table and settled into the chair in the corner, her back to the fire which sat in a square hearth in the middle of the cottage. Eddard sat opposite her, looking at her through the smoke that drifted up to the thatch above their heads.

The smell was good, relaxing him in moments. Nothing bad ever happened at Angela's cottage. It was a law stronger than that which made the tides and the sunrise.

The old woman took her own mug and sipped at it while running her eyes over a half-made woollen blanket that hung from a hook on the wall beside her.

"Should have this finished in time for winter," she said, turning around to face them. "Where are my manners? I'm Angela Mayfield and it's my pleasure to meet you, Jessica. Or should I say Morag?"

Eddard coughed. "I should explain." He gave her the short version of his plan, ending by asking her to help with convincing the abbot that his new companion was the missing princess.

"I think I can help with that," Angela said. "It would be good to have the clan whole again, give two grieving parents their daughter back."

"I'm not their daughter," Jessica said. "You do know that, right?"

Angela laughed. "I ken a few things. Morag was a bonny wee lass, always happy but so mischievous. I bet you're the same. There was the time she tried to steal apples from the tree and fell and broke her arm. Left a wee scar. We were so worried about her but she just laughed, didnae even cry. Hated having to rest while it healed though, demanded apples every day and Cam brought them to her as meek as a lamb. She was loved by both of them, her and her brother."

"She had a brother?"

"Aye, shipped off to a monastery when she went missing. Barely more than a babe in arms. The steward did that though, told them it was for the best. They were too busy grieving to notice. The poor lad didnae ken why they sent him away. I wonder sometimes how he's doing."

"I didn't know he had a brother," Jessica said.

"Not many remember. They're too busy surviving with Ronald taking everything they own to maintain his own good life. I'm wandering, aren't I? You should tell them about breaking your arm, tell them you remember little Philip. He was darker haired than you, two years younger. Had the same blue eyes you have. You'd never convince them for a second if you didn't have those oceans in your eyes, I can tell you that.

"What else? You had started lessons in Latin and writing before you went missing. You could write out the alphabet and proudly used to do it for me back then. You know your parents names, right?"

Jessica shook her head.

"Cam and Rachel. Cam's much like Eddard here, huge and built for smashing down walls but with a smile on him bigger than his temper."

"I dinnae have a temper," Eddard said.

"Not so much anymore."

"Hold on," Jessica said. "Where am I supposed to have been all these years?"

"Tell them the truth. You don't know."

"I don't know? They'll never believe that."

"One look in your eyes and they'll know you're Morag. Now drink up and get gone. I've fishing to do if I'm going to eat tonight."

"Is that enough?" Eddard asked when Morag beckoned him over to the corner. "Does she need to ken anything else?"

Angela took Eddard's hands in her own, squeezing them tightly and lowering her voice. "She is Morag. You get her to the castle and let fate do the rest. You both have a journey to make now and you have been chosen to make it. Take her to the abbot."

Chapter Six

Jessica had a nagging feeling that maybe this wasn't a dream after all. Something about it was too real.

Her imagination wasn't that good. The grass felt so wet against her trousers, the air fresher than any she'd ever known. Not only that but she had a strange sensation of deja vu, as if she'd been here before but that was impossible.

Was she going mad? A tall muscular Highlander like something out of a dream. Long hair, red tartan baldric across his chest. She must be going mad.

Eddard seemed to think so. He said as much before he began marching off in front of her, the rises and falls of the island nothing to him, his pace was constant. She kept slipping on rabbit holes and hidden roots that seemed to lay at perfect ankle breaking height.

Why couldn't he stick to the paths? There were plenty of proper tracks around and yet he was ignoring them all, walking in a perfectly straight line like he was a Roman road, not a person.

He infuriated her but she had no choice but to stick with him. Even if she was going mad, she could see the value of his plan. What choice did she have but to go along with it? It wasn't like she'd be around long enough to deal with the consequences of the truth coming out.

The Laird and Lady would find out sooner or later that she wasn't really their daughter and she wanted to be a long way from here when that happened, ideally about eight hundred years from here.

The thought made her smile. The future. Did she really think she'd traveled back in time? The very idea was insane.

Her hand brushed against a tree trunk as they passed through a copse of oak. It felt so real. As far as she could tell there were two possibilities, neither of which were ideal.

One, she was really here. The laws of time and

space were as realistic as a daytime soap opera. She had actually traveled back in time to the thirteenth century and she was about to go visit the abbot of an abbey on an island in medieval Scotland. In many ways, that was pretty cool. Insane, but cool.

The other alternative was this was a dream. That was a more comfortable thought but she couldn't shake the nagging feeling that this was real. It was all real.

She decided to try and not worry about it. The conclusion was the same either way. She needed to get the key and get home. Do that and whether she was awake or asleep, she would get back home.

The idea had taken on a talismanic quality in her head. It was like the Holy Grail shining out from the top of a castle keep. Get the key and get home. She would not countenance the idea that it might not work, that either she might not get the key or it might not unlock the door to her time. Focus on being Morag. That was what mattered.

What were her parents names? Rachel and Cam. A brother too. Philip. Dark hair. Little brother or big brother? She was already forgetting. She would just have to bluff her way through any tough questions.

It wouldn't be that hard. She was a private

investigator. She was used to lying when she needed to in order to solve a case. It never felt good but sometimes you had to do what you had to do.

And what she had to do was pee.

She ducked down behind a tall clump of bushes. This would be the turning point. Whenever she needed to pee in a dream, she always woke up desperate for the bathroom. Some people jolted awake after falling from a great height. Not her. It was always peeing.

She lowered her trousers, craning her neck up like a meerkat to check he wasn't nearby. Then she took a deep breath and waited to wake up.

It didn't happen. A minute later she was jogging to catch up with Eddard, thinking with a growing sense of certainty that this was real. She really was in the past. She looked at him closely.

Would she imagine such a person? He was so tall and handsome, he looked like a dream man. There was no doubt about it. From his bulging arms to his strongman pecs and that jawline that was to die for.

She could picture herself being swept into his arms and carried off like Scarlett O'Hara. Rhett would not be denied that night. The thought made her grimace. She didn't think like that. She needed neither ravishing nor saving. She needed to get home.

The abbey came into view in the distance just as she rejoined Eddard and as he finally stepped onto a proper path. His pace slowed as he turned and looked at her. "You're tired. Why did you nae tell me?"

"I'm fine."

"Next time, tell me. I can slow."

"Can you?"

"Come on, the gatehouse is around this side."

She looked up at the abbey as they approached. It was in the process of being built. She had no doubt it would be glorious when it was finished. The stone was a dark gray but it was all the more stunning for it, like the church tower had been carved out of solid rock.

The nave was surrounded by wooden scaffolds, men in black cowls working away, scurrying left and right, up and down the ladders. The only sound was that of stone being chiseled.

As she looked a bell rang and at once the men descended, vanishing from sight behind the tall stone wall that shielded the monastery from the rest of the world.

She followed the edge of the wall, doing her

best to keep up with Eddard. He didn't stop until they reached a plain wooden door about a hundred yards further on. He knocked and after a couple of seconds a panel in the door creaked open, a face peering out, eyes narrowed. "Begging for alms is permitted before Prime only. Come back tomorrow."

"We are nae here to plead for pennies. We seek an audience with the abbot."

The panel closed and there was the sound of a bolt being scraped back. The door swung inward a moment later. Eddard ducked to get through and she followed, stepping into a tiny alcove with room for one candle and a stone seat, little protection from the wind or the rain if it should fall.

The monk who'd let them in locked the door once more before turning to face them. "The east guesthouse is empty. You will wait there until brother James is free to see you."

"You have our gratitude," Eddard said, nodding slightly.

The monk turned to Jessica. "You're a woman. Yet you wear hose and your hair is loose." He genuflected before turning away, muttering to himself. "Protect us from Satan, oh Lord, his many temptations he bringeth to bear upon God's children."

"Does he think I'm some evil temptress?" she asked Eddard as they made their way across the grass to the small stone guesthouse.

"Women are not often seen within the abbey grounds. They will let you go no further than the guesthouse. See that wall next to it, that keeps this bit separate from the monks. Only the porter and the abbot get to see the public and wicked temptresses like you."

"How do you know I'm a wicked temptress?"

"You've got that look about you."

"Is that a smile? I think you might be smiling. Have I amused you? Or do you fear I might tempt you into bed as well."

"You wouldnae make me do anything I didnae want to do. I ken how to resist temptation."

"What if I try my seductive seduction techniques of seduction out on you? Seductively?"

"Say seduction more."

"Don't mock me."

"Go on then, how would you seduce me?" he asked, pulling open the door to the guesthouse.

She shrugged. "I'm not sure but I'm sure I could think of something."

They went inside, passing through a narrow corridor and into a sparse room with a fireplace.

The wood was ready to light and Eddard pulled out a flint and steel, striking sparks and bringing the blaze to life while she took the chair by the window. Was that really her? Had she just flirted with someone?

It had to be a dream. She'd never flirted with anyone before. She cringed as she ran her mind over her efforts. No doubt he thought she was some mad woman who needed to be placated in case she went totally over the edge.

"Tell me about yourself," she asked, suddenly aware he was looking at her and had caught her staring. The question was the first thing she could think of to fill the awkward silence.

"What dae you want to ken?"

"How do you know so much about MacGregor castle?"

"Like what?"

"That I won't be able to get in without the steward's approval. What the Lady looks like, Rachel I mean?"

A darkness passed over his face. It was gone in a moment but she saw the pain it brought. Whatever memory it was had hurt him deeply.

"I used to live there, a long time ago. They threw me out."

"What for?"

There was a knock on the door before he could answer. "I'll get it," he said, walking past her. "Another sight of a woman and the whole place might crumble."

She listened as he answered the door. No one spoke but a minute later he returned carrying a wooden tray. On top was half a loaf of dark bread, two apples, and a pitcher of ale with a pair of tankards.

"Abbot's own brew," Eddard said, pouring her out a generous measure. "Legendary this stuff but it rarely gets past the abbey walls. Go on, try it."

She took a sip and it hit her like a freight train. She coughed as it burned a fiery path down her throat. "My goodness, that's ale?"

"Aye. It's good isn't it?" He downed his in one, grinning as he poured out another measure. "Nectar of the Gods."

She managed another sip without coughing. She felt more relaxed at once, the fiery spirit warming her insides. The tension she'd felt since arriving here fell away in stages until she was almost slouched in her chair, letting the flames in the hearth warm her toes further.

The dew from the grass had soaked through her

shoes and she was glad of the heat. And the ale. The more she drank, the more she wanted.

"You better get some bread in you to soak it up," he said, lifting her head by the chin as she began to doze. "It wouldnae do for the abbot to see you soused like this."

"We could tell him Morag's an alcoholic," she said, noticing how hard it was to concentrate on saying words. Why were words so difficult? They never used to be.

She took the hunk of bread he offered and tried to bite into it. Rock hard, it almost broke her teeth.

"Not like that," he said, dipping his own portion into his ale. "Like this. Soak it first."

She nodded, losing her bread in her tankard and having to fish it out while he watched her, his shoulders shaking as he held in a laugh. "What?" she asked, pouting at him. "Am I amusing you?"

"Nae, not at all."

Another knock on the door and she waved her hand in the air. "You may answer that for me."

"Yes, my Lady," he said with a huge bow, leaving her alone to giggle to herself. She could get used to ale like this.

She'd never been a big drinker. An occasional wine to celebrate solving a case was about all she ever let herself enjoy. This was something else. She felt as if every muscle in her body were loosening, all the knots in her shoulders coming undone. Much more and she might melt into a puddle on the floor.

Eddard came back in with two steaming pitchers. "What's that?" she asked as he set them down on the table near the fire. "Boiling oil for the temptress?"

"Hot water for us to wash before the abbot sees us."

He was already pushing his hose down and she barely had time to turn away before it was off. With her back to him she listened to the sound of splashing water. "You could have asked me to give you some privacy," she said, staring pointedly at the wall in front of her.

"I've nothing tae hide," he replied.

"Yes you have."

"What?"

"That," she said, pointing behind her. "Put it away."

More splashing and she was sure she could hear him chuckling to himself. "You can turn around now," he said a minute later. She spun in her chair and couldn't help looking down. His hose clung to him. He hadn't bothered to dry himself. The fabric showed the outline of his…

"You need to get a wash," he said. "You've the dust of that rockfall all over you. The abbot willnae see you like that."

"I'm not washing in front of you."

"Och, you're a precious one, my Lady, aren't you?"

"Go on. Out you go."

She waved her hand in the air and he went, smiling as he did so. She glanced at the corridor to make sure he was out of sight before standing up, feeling decidedly dizzy at once. She wobbled left then right as the floor sloped away from her then it turned vertical then back to flat.

With her arms outstretched she waited for the dizziness to pass. A cold draft hit her from the corridor and she shivered, lifting her tankard to take another sip. The warmth hit her at once and her inhibitions receded like the outgoing tide.

A minute later she was stripped to the waist and dipping her hand into the pitcher. "Ouch," she yelped, pulling her hand away. The water was boiling hot.

"What's wrong?" Eddard asked, appearing in the doorway a second later.

"Get out!" she shouted, grabbing hold of her chest. "Now!"

"You cried out. What's the matter?"

"It was just hot. Now go."

He went but as he did so she noticed his eyes glancing down at her chest. She didn't move until he was out of sight and even then she kept glancing at the door to make sure he wasn't coming back.

More tentatively this time, she dipped her fingers into the water, doing the best she could to clean herself without a cloth or towel.

She wanted to wash her hair but with no shampoo she knew that would be a mistake. If they thought her hair was wild now, wait until they saw it drying out with no help. She'd look like she'd been struck by lightning.

She looked down at her body while she washed the dirt from it. Had he liked what he saw?

Where did that thought come from? What did she care what he thought? He should have been ashamed of looking, that was what she should be thinking.

She'd looked at him too.

She had no choice though and she'd looked away as soon as she realized, trying not to think of the hose sliding down off his hips, nor what she would have seen if she'd kept looking that way.

Her mouth felt dry all of a sudden but she didn't want any more ale. Her head was starting to hurt. With no towel she had to dry herself using the heat of the fire and it was some time before she called to him. The last bubbles of alcohol popped out of her soul and disappeared with the steam from the water.

Edward returned and looked like he was about to say something when there was a knock at the door.

"What now?" she asked. "Stylist? Make up artist?"

Eddard headed down the corridor and she glanced after him, seeing him step aside to let a monk enter. The two of them joined her by the fire-place and only then did the monk pull back his cowl to reveal a friendly wrinkled face crowned by graying hair a similar color to the stone of the abbey walls.

"Good day," the monk said, giving her a curt nod. "My name is brother James. I believe you wished to see me."

"I bring you great news," Eddard said. "Morag

has returned and we need your boat to take her back home where she belongs."

"So she has," James said, taking her hands in his and examining her closely, his expression cold. "You have your mother's eyes. Tell me, my dear. If I were to sing to you, I left my baby lying here, how would you reply?"

Jessica frowned as the words came out of her mouth without her giving them a moment's thought. "Lying here, lying here. I left my baby lying here."

"Extraordinary," James said, letting her hands go. "Your mother used to sing that to you to help you sleep. But where have you been all these years?"

"I dinnae ken," she said, doing her best to manage a Scottish accent, finding it easier than she expected.

"She lost her memory," Eddard said, jumping in to save her. "She washed up on the shore this morning. I knew it was her at once."

"Of course it is," James said with a warm smile that made guilt drip straight into Jessica's heart. He was so trusting and she was lying to his face. A man of God. Would she go to hell for this? "Take her to the Laird and Lady at once. I have no doubt they will rejoice. The bells will peal to celebrate your return, my girl. May God be praised. I will recall Philip from his cell in the low country."

"I should douse the fire," Eddard said.

"Leave me to do that. There is no time to waste. The boat is in the boathouse. Brother Richard will take you down to it. Hallelujah!"

Jessica let Eddard lead her outside. With the door closed behind them he turned and grinned at her. "We did it!"

He threw his arms around her and she felt the warmth of his body burn into her much quicker and deeper than the ale had done. She let him hold her. "We did it," she echoed back to him.

He pulled back and looked like he was about to kiss her. She closed her eyes automatically but then his touch was gone. When she looked he was heading for the gatehouse, not looking back at her.

She tried not to be disappointed. She tried to be angry that he had assumed he might kiss her at all. The anger wouldn't come. Instead, the question that bounced around her head as they were escorted to the boat was, did he like what he saw?

Chapter Seven

While the monk untied the ropes holding the boat in place, Eddard looked across at Jessica. She was looking at him with a strange expression on her face. He couldn't place it.

Was it hatred? Disgust? Anger? Her lips were pursed together like she was concentrating on something. Had he really been so close to kissing those lips? What had come over him?

It wasn't like he could blame the abbot's ale. He had handled a half a barrel of the stuff before. Last year at the harvest festival they'd celebrated the first decent crop in years with the monks, all of them in it together as the famine slowly came to an end.

That was the last good time he could remember.

It was mere days later that the missive came. Ronald was raising the tithe on grinding, conveniently in time for the glut of wheat they had. By the time he'd taken his cut, they were worse off than during the famine.

His fists clenched by his sides. He wanted to wrap his hands around the steward's neck, choke the life out of him. He wanted to do it for the people of the clan, not just for his own base instincts. Get rid of the steward and their lives would be immeasurably better off.

Jessica looked away. She was watching the monk's deft hands working the ropes. He examined her closely. Why had he wanted to kiss her? If he was going to talk about base instincts, why not start with that?

There was something about her that was bugging him. If only he could work it out. Maybe he'd have been better off as a monk. Perhaps they were right. Women were a distraction.

He suppressed a smile as the last of the ropes came undone. She was a distraction. She was going to distract the Laird and Lady long enough for him to get into the treasury and get what was his.

The family coffers had been confiscated when he'd been exiled, taken into the safekeeping of the

Laird and Lady. He knew what that meant. Ronald would claim them as his own. He could only hope the fiend hadn't spent them all yet.

"God be with you," the monk muttered to him before turning and heading out of the boathouse, leaving him alone with Jessica.

"Can you row?" he asked her.

She shook her head. "I can give it a go."

"Never mind. You sit at that end and dinnae rock it, understand? The waters are deep here."

He held out a hand and she took it, using him to balance against as she climbed into the boat. He clambered in and took the oars, using the end to push them out of the boathouse. The current took them at once as they drifted slowly out from the shore.

"We need to work our way around to the west," Eddard said, pushing the oars into the water, enjoying the strain on his muscles. It felt like they were coming to life. He'd always loved rowing but hadn't been in a boat for years, not since Ronald's guard on the water tripled in size.

They were lucky for the first ten minutes. He saw no one else. He'd even begun to think they might make it to the far shore without any trouble. Was that too much to hope for?

He looked at Jessica while they made their way slowly across to the mainland. She was trying not to look back at him, glancing his way and then moving to look out at the distant mountains instead. He said nothing. It didn't really matter what she was thinking. What mattered was her upholding her end of the bargain.

The more he looked at her, the more he could convince himself she was Morag. Her hair was the same color as Rachel's and just as unwieldy. She had the same button nose but those eyes held the killer blow. He could happily drown in those eyes.

"What is this key?"

"Huh?" She looked at him as if waking up. "What did you say?"

"This key you're after. What is it?"

"It's a key," she said with a shrug.

"There must be something special about it. Tell me."

"You wouldn't believe me if I did."

"Try me."

She shrugged again. "What the heck. I got a key sent to me in the mail along with a flyer for MacGregor Castle."

"What's a flyer?"

"Like an advertisement. Never mind. I took the

key with me to the castle and I heard this woman singing on the other side of the door to the Laird's bedroom.

"I unlocked it and I don't know what happened but then I was suddenly on the battlements and two men in armor were dragging me into this room.

"Then this sleazy fat guy turned up, took the key off me and used it to unlock another door. He shoved me through and kept the key."

"And that's where I found you?"

"You don't believe me, do you."

"I ken you appeared out of nowhere at the abbey. I ken you look exactly like Morag and have got everyone believing you are her. Even Angela seemed convinced and we told her who you really are."

"I promise I'm not making this up."

"Maybe you are and maybe you aren't. What will you do if we manage to get this key of yours back?"

"Go home. What about you?"

"What about me?"

"What will you do when we get to the castle?"

"Help you find the key."

She frowned, leaning forward in her seat. "What's in it for you?"

"I told you before. If the Laird and Lady come out of hiding, they'll see what harm their cursed steward has been daeing tae the clan. He waited a long time to take over and he's made the most of it but time's up."

"No, there's more to it. There's something you're not telling me."

"I dinnae ken what you're blethering about."

He noticed too late that there was something behind her shoulder. He cursed himself for getting distracted by the conversation when he should have been watching.

"What's that?" she asked, seeing the expression on his face. "What have you seen?"

"Ronald's guards. See if there are any cowls down by your feet."

"There's nothing in here."

"Then we're going tae have tae outrow them. Haud on." He began pulling at the oars faster but they had a sail and the wind was in their favor.

From what he could make out, there were half a dozen of them on board. Two minding the sail and the rudder, the others with bows ready. They were getting closer.

He glanced behind him at the mainland which still seemed far too distant. Could they make it? He knew in his heart they had no chance but they had to try. "Duck," he said. "Lest they start loosing off."

She slid down the boat until she was at his feet and just in time. Arrows began hitting the water around them, the sound like seagulls diving for fish. One whipped past too close. There was only one chance to end this without both of them being killed.

Lifting one oar into the boat, he shoved the other deep into the water, their vessel turning quickly as Jessica grabbed onto the sides. "What are you doing?" she yelled.

"Whatever I can," he replied.

The guards hadn't expected that and they had no time to maneuver out the way. The flimsy rowing boat crashed into the side of their ship, knocking the archers off balance.

Eddard was up and into their boat in a second, swinging the oar from left to right. A sword jabbed at him from behind but he ignored it. There would be time to deal with it shortly. First he had to redress the balance.

The oar cracked an archer on the head. As the man fell into the water, Eddard swung at the man beside him, catching him an almighty blow in the stomach. That was two thrashing in the depths.

He spun on his heels and shifted the oar over his head, rewarded by a crunch behind him. Turning he saw the third man go in and the fourth was just notching an arrow when he stabbed the oar onto his feet, breaking at least three of his toes.

The man yelled and leaped back, giving Eddard room to shove him off. Two left, both armed with swords. They lunged, catching him on the chest but he leaned back enough to turn fatal blows into glancing ones.

Blood poured freely as he smacked the swords away with the oar, taking tiny steps backward, keeping them both in view.

"Oi!" Jessica shouted from the remains of the rowing boat.

One glanced back at her as she hurled a broken piece of wood at him. It did no harm but knocked him off balance and gave Eddard all the chance he needed.

He dropped the oar and sprinted forward, catching the blade in his hand, letting it cut him but not releasing his grip. With his shoulder down he shoved hard and the man went into the water, leaving Eddard with the sword.

He flipped it in the air, catching it by the handle and turning to the last man who took one look at the odds before leaping out of the boat into the water, swimming away for his life.

Eddard caught hold of Jessica just as the rowing boat sank beneath the waves, lifting her into the sailboat. "You're bleeding," she said. "Let me look at you."

"Not yet," he said, turning the ropes that held the sail, ignoring the pain in his hands. "We need some distance. They may want another round."

The boat began to move toward the shore, leaving the cursing men to spit and shake their fists at him from the water. Only when they were specks in the distance did he let himself relax. The shore was minutes away. They had made it.

He staggered, almost falling. That wasn't like him. Blinking the fuzziness away from his eyes he concentrated on the ropes, guiding them closer to the mainland. At last it was there.

Ten feet away.

Five.

The boat hit the shore and scraped the bottom, throwing the two of them to their knees. She was up first and he had to work hard to get back onto his feet. His limbs felt heavier than ever.

"Let me look at you," she said again. "Sit down."

"We have to keep moving," he said, grabbing her hand and pulling her away from the shore. "They'll be after us in greater numbers soon. Time is our only help. We must be inland before they make it to shore. Then you can look at me all you want."

"You'll never make it thirty miles to the castle. You're bleeding too much you stubborn fool."

"We dinnae need to make it thirty. We need to make it five."

"Five? What's in five miles?"

"The Dog and Fox."

"What's that?"

"A tavern run by a friend of mine. Get there and we can hide out the night."

He took one last look behind him, gratified to see no one swimming nearby. The vision blurred and he had to blink it clear. They had cut him worse than he thought. Still, there would be time to tend to his wounds when they were safe.

He turned his back to the loch and together they headed in land in search of the tavern, and the safety it represented. He staggered and would have fallen if Jessica didn't take his arm and let him lean on her.

"This tavern better not be far," she said, glancing down at the blood soaking into his baldric.

He winced as pain lanced through him. "Come on," he said through gritted teeth. "Let's get moving."

Chapter Eight

T he lights shining out from the tavern
were the only spots of yellow in an otherwise black landscape.

As the sun had set clouds rolled across the sky,
turning a dark night into the blackest Jessica had
ever known. It was so dark she kept seeing movement out of the corner of her eye, flashes within
her brain trying to create something out of
nothing.

She could barely see Eddard and for that she
was grateful. He had begun to mumble to himself
as they walked, words that meant nothing to her.
Was he talking in Gaelic? Old English? She had no
idea.

He tripped time and again while trying to

march and she'd had to force him to slow down and focus on giving her directions.

How he could tell his way in the dark with so much blood loss, she had no idea. She prayed he did know the way because otherwise they were about as lost as two people could be.

When she saw the lights in the distance, tiny twinkling specks that shifted and faded and then glowed once again, she felt a wave of relief washing over her.

Even if it wasn't the tavern, it would be somewhere they could stop and she could examine his injuries properly. He had at least two sword cuts to the chest and his hand had been slippery with blood whenever she helped him up from yet another fall.

"The tavern," he said, standing upright for the first time since the sun had set. "There." He pointed toward the light and it was as if the life came back into him. He began to march again and she had to jog to keep up. The terrain underfoot was smooth. They were on a track of some kind. It wouldn't take long to get there.

Within half an hour the lights grew big enough for her to make out what they were, candles and a glowing fire visible through open windows. She could hear voices talking, laughter echoing out from inside. The building was smaller than bars in her time but it was all the more welcome after a trek through the dark with an injured man.

It seemed to have taken the last of Eddard's strength to reach the tavern. He shoved the door open and fell into the nearest chair, head on his chest. She followed, getting a proper look at him.

It wasn't as bad as she'd first feared. The wounds in his chest had stopped bleeding. Keep him warm and the edges clean and they should mend themselves. She was more concerned about his hand. Each time he'd fallen he'd reopened the cuts across his fingers and they needed covering if she was going to stop any more blood loss.

She barely noticed the faces staring at her as she crossed to the makeshift counter near the back wall. Behind it a man was hefting an empty barrel onto his shoulder, turning away to carry it through a swinging door.

"Hey," she said. "I need help."

"And I need to get this barrel away and a fresh one out." He continued walking.

"I need a cloth. Have you got a rag or something and some hot water?"

"Haud on." He pushed through the door and disappeared. She looked back at Eddard. He was slumping down on the chair, blood still dripping from his hand.

"I haven't got time for this," she said, stepping around the corner and following the landlord through the door.

"Oi!" he said as she snatched a cloth from the wall. "You can't be back here."

"Hot water," she said, her eyes narrowing. "Now."

He paled at the expression on her face, nodding and turning away. "Over here."

She watched as he dipped a tankard into a huge steaming cauldron. For some reason she thought of the witches of Macbeth. Hubble, bubble, toil, and trouble.

She took the pitcher from the landlord and rushed back through to the other room. Kneeling in front of Eddard she dipped the cloth into the water, soaking it for as long as she dared, wishing she had access to a pharmacy or a decent hospital, just this once.

With the cloth burning her fingers she wrapped it around his hand. He stirred, looking up at her, blinking, his eyes coming back into focus.

"I like you," he said. "You're a decent lass. I like you. I. Like. You. Like you."

"You like me," she replied, knotting the cloth in place. "Got it. Just keep still for a minute."

She waited, watching the cloth and holding her breath for what felt like forever. Blood began to soak through it but then it stopped. Only water was dripping to the floor anymore.

"Keep that still," she said, lifting Eddard's chin, watching his eyes come back into focus again. "Got it?"

He nodded. "I like you." A grin spread across his face as his eyes closed again.

She returned to the kitchen, grabbing another length of cloth from the hook on the wall, bringing it back to Eddard. She cleaned the wounds on his chest carefully while he mumbled about liking her.

She smiled. If only it were true, not the ramblings of a man on the brink of losing consciousness. She wouldn't mind him liking her. There would be worse things than a six foot plus man mountain taking care of her, acting like a guardian angel. Maybe more.

It wasn't true though and she knew better than to think it was. She cleaned his wounds as best she could, moving his baldric to one side to ensure she got every spot she needed to.

When she was done she hoisted herself into the

chair opposite him and watched. He was snoring loudly. Was that a good sign? She wasn't sure.

"Eddard?" a voice said above her. She looked up to find the landlord standing with his arms folded, staring at the two of them. "Well, well, well. Still getting into scrapes, I see."

Eddard grunted, his eyes blinking open. "Scott. Get me a drink or the Devil take you."

"You havenae paid me for the broken window last time you were in here."

"Och, you owe me for getting rid of those wolves, I'd say we're even. Or would you rather I'd let them run riot?" He was sitting up in his chair, the blank expression gone as the color returned to his cheeks.

The landlord rolled his eyes before smiling. "It's good to see you again. Ronald ended your banishment, has he?"

"Not quite."

"So you're on the lam? I like it."

"Listen, Scott. Have you got a room for the night?"

"And I suppose you want to stay for free?"

"I'll be able to pay you in a couple of days."

"That's what you said last time and it's been what? Ten years?"

"Trust you to remember that far back. Look, can we stay or not?"

The landlord nodded. "Aye, you can stay but I've only one room."

Eddard shook his head, folding his arms over his chest and wincing as he brushed over his wounds. "The lass cannae stay with me. We are not newlyweds."

"It's that or out the door. Market day tomorrow. I'm full up."

Eddard turned to Jessica. "What do you want to do?"

"We'll share," she said. "Don't look at me like that. I don't snore."

Scott led them through a door near the fireplace and up a narrow flight of stairs. The sound of talking followed them up, only becoming muffled when they walked into the far room and looked about them.

"This is fine," Jessica said, turning to the landlord. "Thank you."

"Take care of him," Scott replied. "Until I get paid, at least."

"I will do that," she said as he pulled the door closed, leaving the two of them alone.

"You take the bed," Eddard said. "I'll go by the fire." He began pulling blankets over to the floor.

"You're wounded," she replied, stepping in front of him. "You sleep on the bed. That's an order."

"My honor willnae allow a lass to sleep at my feet like a pup."

"And I won't see a wounded man sleeping on the floor."

He shrugged. "Then I guess we'll just have to share."

He pulled the blankets back, wincing as he climbed into the bed. "Come on, it's going to get cold when the fire dies."

She looked at him, thinking that if this was a dream, she would have to wake up soon. How long had she been here? She climbed in slowly, trying not to tense up. Lying perfectly still on her back, she looked up at the thatch above her head. A cold draft blew in from under the door, making her shiver.

At once his arm was around her, drawing her back against him, his mouth an inch from the back of her neck. She thought she'd feel tense but she didn't. She felt safe, protected, and warm. His heat was taking the chill from her bones and within minutes her eyes grew heavy.

If this was a dream, she would wake up any moment. She could feel herself falling for the burly Highlander. He wasn't real though. She knew that for sure. Yet, he felt so very real.

She jolted upright in bed. She'd been dreaming. Was she back home? What had the dream been about? The old nightmare. Walking through a door, a different door to the one that brought her here. She was little. A hand was on the door. Then she was trapped.

Hammering to get out. She closed her eyes, wanting to return to the dream despite her fear, knowing if she could go back often enough, eventually she'd find out what it meant.

What had woken her? Something was out there. She heard the creak of a floorboard and a rustling sound. As her eyes adjusted to the dark she realised she was still in the tavern. This was real. Her heart sank as she tried to accept that. Her brain hurt.

Fear began to rise inside her. She reached back to tap Eddard, to make sure he was still there, but he was gone. She almost cried out when a hand covered to her lips but then she realized it was him.

"Shush," he hissed. "Dinnae make a sound," he continued. "There are four of them trying to build up the courage to come in. Here, hold this."

She felt something cold and sharp in her hand. He'd given her a dagger. "I can't use this," she hissed.

"You might have to," he replied.

Then he was gone. She looked for him in the darkness but he'd vanished into the shadows. She waited, listening hard, the dagger gripped tight in her hand. She wished she could wake up but no matter how hard she tried, the world remained real.

Was she about to die? Who was coming for them? Was it more men like on the loch. They'd barely escaped that encounter. What chance of getting lucky twice in a row?

The sound in the corridor died away. From the next room she could hear loud snoring but nothing else. She began to hope they might have gone, that the danger was passed.

Then the door crashed open.

She heard rather than saw what happened next. Crashes, cries, muffled shouts and thuds. It lasted less than a minute and then there was a flare of flame and a candle was lit near the door, guttering but then glowing into life.

The yellow glare it provided made her gasp. Three men lay dead on the floor. Eddard was standing among them, his sword dripping with blood.

"You said there were four," she said. "Where's the other one?"

"Here," a voice said behind her. A cold blade pressed to her throat an instant later. She was dragged to her feet as Eddard bristled, his sword hand itching to move.

"You should have stayed on your island," her captor said. "Put the sword down and you won't have to see her innards spilled. Would be a shame to ruin such a pretty one."

"All right," Eddard replied, letting his sword drop to the ground. "Now let her go."

"You really are a fool," the man said, lifting the dagger from Jessica's throat. He went to throw it but as he flicked his arm, she shoved him backward as hard as she could.

He let out a scream and she spun on the spot in time to see him crashing through the flimsy shutters to fall from sight. She ran to the window and looked out. He was dead, having landed on his head in the yard below.

"Wait here," Eddard said.

He ran from the room and she thought about obeying him but then she looked down at the corpses, blood spreading across the floorboards under them. She crept out of the room, descending the stairs, stopping halfway when she heard voices.

Leaning down she was able to peep into the main room. Eddard had the landlord up against the wall, sword pressed into his ribs. "How much did they pay you?" he was asking. "Was it worth it?"

"Please," Scott begged, spitting his words out. "Dinnae kill me."

"Was it worth it?"

"We can split it, fifty-fifty, just listen to me a minute."

"Split what? What are you talking about?"

"Ronald wants her dead. He offered two pounds of gold for her body brought back to him."

"What? What does he want her for?"

"I dinnae ken but what does it matter. Think of it, Eddard. A pound of gold. You could set up your own kingdom with that much."

"He hasnae got that much gold."

"He will have. He's going to rob the tax train when it comes through."

Eddard laughed. "And you believe him? You're more of a fool than I thought."

"You need the money, I ken you do."

"I'll get my money back out of the treasury and

that's all I'll take. The tax train? That's a fool's errand."

"That's what I said but he's hired Vikings to the job."

Jessica noticed something Eddard hadn't. While they were talking the landlord had reached into his pocket and was drawing out a knife of his own.

"Look out!" she screamed.

Eddard saw it just in time, the blade catching his skin but only nicking him. He roared with anger as the landlord lunged a second time. Jessica looked around her, seeing a tankard on the nearest table. Jumping down the stairs she grabbed it and hurled it through the air.

It missed entirely, hitting the wall behind the landlord. She gasped as it bounced off and fell onto his head, sending him staggering straight onto Eddard's outstretched sword.

"Come on," Eddard said, pulling his sword free and turning to Jessica. "It isnae safe here anymore. We'll find somewhere else to sleep."

They ran for the door and out into the darkness, not stopping until they were both fighting for breath.

"Where are we?" she asked, looking out into the

darkness, hearing only water running in the distance, nothing else.

"Near the river," he replied, still pulling her forward.

"That's helpful."

"There's a barn over there. Hidden from view if I remember right. We'll stop there."

They turned off the track and passed through a pasture, descending slowly before stopping in front of a stone building that had appeared from nowhere.

"Is it safe?" she asked as he looked inside.

"Aye. Been empty many years. I dare not light a fire though. We will have to sleep close if we are to keep warm."

"I can live with that," she replied.

"Here," he said, passing her something in the dark. "Drink this."

"When did you get that?" she asked, feeling the leather flask in her hand, fluid sloshing around inside.

"Snatched it off the table when we ran," he replied.

She took a swig of the contents, the strength of it almost knocking her off her feet. "Alcohol was stronger back then," she said with a cough. "Wowsers."

She felt dizzy but warmed by the spirit, sinking to the musty old straw at her feet.

Eddard took the flask and gulped down half of it, kicking off more straw to form a kind of blanket. Together they settled under it, his arm once more around her as she tried to sleep. Rest wouldn't come.

Eddard cursed. "I cannae believe Scott took that blaggard's money. See what poverty does to a clan? Friends turn on friends. And I killed him. What does that say about me?"

"You didn't ask for it," she replied. She turned to look at him in the dark. "Do you know what you were saying to me when we got to the tavern?"

"What?"

"I like you."

"No I didnae."

"You did, you kept saying it over and over."

"Well, so what? I do like you."

His grip on her tightened and she turned away once more. Could she tell him about what happened all those years ago? The reason why she never kissed a man.

That wasn't true though, was it? She had kissed

a man. She'd been a girl in foster care and he'd been in charge of the place. It sickened her to recall it. Him holding her face while she tried to get away.

She shuddered and he took it as her becoming chilled, his arm holding her tighter against him.

She couldn't tell him. She couldn't tell anyone. It didn't matter. This was a dream and she'd wake up or this was real and she'd go home. Either way, no point sharing her dirty little secrets.

She closed her eyes, willing herself to sleep. She found herself thinking again about what he'd said, about how she felt while he held her. How safe she felt. There was still that tension though, would that ever leave her?

Oh, to be normal. To not have a past more murky than the filth underneath the straw. While she was wishing, why not wish for a horse with wings to fly her back to her enormous palace in the Bahamas?

Exhaustion washed over her as her aching limbs throbbed painfully. Before she knew what was happening, she was asleep, dreaming once again of being trapped behind a door. On the other side, though she could not see, she knew there stood a man with an M scarred into the back of his hand.

Chapter Nine

E ddard woke up aching all over. He sat up in the darkness, listening hard. Nothing. If they were looking for him, they were looking in the wrong places, following the false trails he'd laid.

He ran through a mental checklist. Injuries? Bad but not fatal. The fact that he was alive was always a good sign. He tapped his chest. The wounds hadn't reopened overnight. That was good. The cut Scott had given him with the dagger had crusted over. It stung but didn't feel as if it was going to rot.

His hand was the worst of all the injuries. Each time he clenched or loosened his fist, pain shot up his arm.

He was used to pain. He could handle it. The only question was whether it would affect his ability to fight. There was no way of answering that until it happened. He would just have to wait and see.

He thought back to the fight on the boat. Did he have a choice but to use his hand to grab the sword? It was a spur of the moment thing and it had ended the fight but while the guards would soon dry, he would be dealing with the consequences for some time.

He sat up silently, moving out of the straw like morning mist when the dawn began, rising without sound and drifting outside.

He scanned the gray pre-dawn landscape. He made a mental calculation. If they marched hard and managed without too many stops, they could make MacGregor Castle by nightfall. That would give him the night to check the outsides, see where the guards roamed, see if the routines had changed in patrolling since he was last there.

Would she be able to walk that far? When he first met her he would have been certain she couldn't manage it but she'd surprised him. She'd surprised him a lot. Warning him about Scott. That had saved him.

The wounds had dulled his attention. He should

have noticed the knife but he didn't until it was almost too late. The sting above his hips was his payment for that.

She had run when he'd run, she hadn't complained about being tired despite the distance they'd traveled. She had tended to his wounds with knowledge he had not expected.

If she was going to make it, she would need something to eat though. So would he. He scanned the ground, moving swiftly over it until he found what he was looking for.

He returned to the barn a few minutes later. She still slept. He had to wake her. They needed to eat and then get moving. He stood in the doorway, watching her for a moment. Her face looked troubled even in sleep.

She was muttering something to herself. "I dinnae want to go through the door. Where's Ma and Da?"

She looked pretty in the straw despite her twisting and grimacing as the dream took her. Not that it mattered what she looked like.

What mattered was getting her to the castle and getting into the treasury. Then he could boot out Ronald and what happened after that would be up to the spirits of the Highlands.

"No! Let me out!" she yelled, sitting bolt upright and opening her eyes. She blinked several times, running her hands through her hair. "Where am I?"

"In the barn with me," he said, kneeling beside her. "Here, eat this."

"I'm not a rabbit," she said, looking down at the green pile at her feet. "Is that grass?"

"It's hawthorn leaves, best I can do for now."

"No bacon and eggs?" She yawned loudly. "Cup of coffee?"

"There may be better food when we get to the castle."

"The castle. Oh, goodness. I'm still here, aren't I. This isn't a dream. I'm really here." She picked up a couple of the leaves and ate them, tossing her hair back a moment later. "Then I suppose we better get going."

Once again he marveled at her. He'd never known anyone like her. She could go from despair to determination in the blink of an eye. She was on her feet a moment later. "How long to the castle?"

"About twenty miles from here if we cut through the mountain pass."

"Then we go that way."

"How good's your climbing."

"Good enough. How long will this take?"

"If they weren't looking for us, I'd have said two days but we need to move swiftly. If news gets back to the castle that we're on the move, Ronald will have his entire guard out looking for us. Dinnae forget you've a bounty on your head."

"I meant to ask yesterday, why does he want me dead?"

"I dinnae ken but I bet it's got something to do with that key of yours. Kill you and no one kens what it can do."

"You know."

"Aye and I'll be dead by your side if he has his way."

She stuffed the last few leaves in her mouth. "I'd kill for a coffee and a donut."

"You do talk strange sometimes, lass."

"So do you. Now are we walking or are we talking all morning?"

He suppressed a laugh. "Yes, my Lady." With an exaggerated bow, he backed out of the barn. She followed him in time to see the sun rising over the distant mountains.

"Tell me those aren't the ones we're going to climb."

"Nae," he said, taking hold of her shoulders

and turning her to face the opposite direction. "Those ones."

"Oh," she said, looking at the soaring peaks in front of them both. "Fine."

The journey took longer than he expected. It wasn't just the wind which blew directly into their faces, slowing them down. It was his injuries. For the first time he was aware of his age, of how long he'd spent in exile.

He hadn't really thought about his body aging before but the wounds which he might have laughed at when he was younger were plaguing him and draining his energy. He said nothing about them, slowing only when absolutely necessary.

They stopped twice. The first time he managed to catch a rabbit but it had little enough meat to sustain the two of them, not helped by the size of the fire upon which he cooked.

The wind kept sending the flames down to the ground and even with a stone wall to shelter against, there was never enough heat to sear the animal properly.

The second time he stood alone while Jessica went behind a clump of bushes to relieve herself. He rubbed his aching muscles while she was out of sight, bringing them back to life.

His hand had stopped sending pain shooting up his arm but the tiredness he felt was out of all proportion to the length of the march. Was it the injuries or the wind? Or perhaps because it had been a long time since he'd needed to march this far. He was clearly out of shape.

That would change when they got to the castle and he got his life back. When Jessica emerged, she looked pale. She was trembling slightly. "Are you cold?" he asked.

"No," she replied. "Just frightened."

They began to walk again, making their way slowly upward toward the mountain range. "It will be fine," he said after a moment's silence.

He was less sure than he sounded. There was a chance they'd be picked off by archers before they even made it inside. What they needed was some kind of disguise. He filed that thought for the future. For now, focus on getting there.

The land grew more familiar as they scrambled up the mountain side to the pass that looked like a cut from a giant's sword, running through the range and gradually down the other side.

The two of them lapsed into silence for longer and longer, the conversation dying. He thought about asking her more about the key, about why she thought this was a dream, but he decided against it.

If he got to know her too well, it would only make it harder when they parted. And part they would, one way or another. Either she'd be locked in the dungeon as an imposter or she'd get that key of hers, open her magic door, and vanish from his life.

He thought about her being imprisoned and tried to ignore the guilt that washed over him. Could he do that to her? Would he not be better off abandoning the plan?

He shook his head. No, what good would that do? Ronald would ruin the clan, maybe the whole country if he managed to ambush the tax train and steal the coffers for himself.

She'd be stuck where she least wanted to be, forever yearning to get back to her world, wherever it was. Behind a door. That was it. Behind a door he could not walk through for it belonged to her alone. That he knew though he had no idea how.

He thought hard while they made their way to the castle. When it finally came into view in the distance the sun was setting. He allowed them to stop for a minute. She sank to the ground and lay back, stretching her arms out and yawning.

He stood stock still, looking at the turrets he feared he might never see her again. They were hard to see from this distance in such low light but he knew their outline like he knew his own soul.

The castle was part of him. Was that part of the battlement missing? It had jagged edges like it had collapsed. Was he too late to prevent the ruin of the place?

The Laird would never have let the place decay if he were aware of it. He felt a flare of anger. It was one thing to grieve their missing child but did that give them the right to ignore their people's plight? Or had the steward dripped poison in their ears, made them feel her loss was their fault?

He swallowed the anger. It was his bitterness at his exile that was coloring his thoughts. They had left their steward in charge as many Lairds did during illness or travel. He was the one who was burning the very world around him to keep himself entertained.

It didn't make much sense though. Ronald had always been dull, easily led by others. He wasn't the type to make these kinds of decisions without someone telling him to.

Eddard had wondered about this before but

he'd stopped himself thinking too much about it for fear the anger would swallow him entirely.

He could never shake the feeling that someone else was pulling the steward's strings, someone lurking in the shadows where no one could see them. Who might it be? Another Laird? A Norman? Maybe a Viking?

"What now," Jessica asked, sitting up on her elbows. "Full frontal assault? Or would you rather attack the castle?"

He managed a smile. "I doubt you could handle a full frontal assault from me?"

"Oh, getting cocky are we? I bet I could handle you."

"Time for that later," he said, marvelling once more at how quickly she could distract him from his own thoughts. "We get a little closer but not too close."

"Us or the castle?"

"The castle."

"Of course. Why not go down now?"

He raised his eyebrows.

"To the castle," she said, blushing slightly and slapping his leg.

He laughed before turning to again look at the turrets in the distance. Torches were being lit. Soon it would be too dark to see much of anything. "They never let anyone in at night. We will have to approach at dawn."

"Will they even let us inside?"

"We'll see. Come on, we shall find shelter somewhere."

As they descended the hillside into a broad valley, tiredness again swept over him. A small cottage stood alone about a quarter of a mile ahead. It looked close to collapse. It had looked far different in the past. "We shall see if Drummond and his wife still reside there."

They made it to the cottage just in time. Above their heads the rain which had threatened all day came down in a sudden torrent. Even the torches on the castle walls struggled against it.

Eddard hammered on the door of the cottage. "I have a sheep to sell," he called out.

The door scraped open. "The last boy who tried to sell me my own sheep got a clip around the ear for his trouble."

The old man standing in the entrance suddenly smiled, the warmth lighting up his watery eyes. "Eddard MacGregor, as I live and breathe."

"You remember me then, Drummond?"

"Who could forget the boy who killed Ronald's

brother? Couldn't you have run the steward through as well, save us all a world of trouble? And who's this?"

"Let us in out this rain and we shall tell you."

"Of course, where are my manners. In you come, both of you?"

Once inside, Eddard saw Maggie under the covers in the corner by the fire. Her eyes were closed.

"She sleeps most times now," Drummond said by way of explanation. "What she needs is an apothecary but there are none at the castle anymore."

"Where did they go?"

"All went in search of better food elsewhere. Ronald will be the death of us all."

"Aye, but perhaps not for much longer. Recognize the lass?"

Drummond squinted in the low light of the cottage, examining Jessica closely. "Jings, it's the spitting image of Rachel."

"It's Morag, back from her travels."

"Praise the Lord." The man pumped Jessica's hand up and down. "Morag, by God, it's good to see you once more."

"Halloo," Jessica replied in a decent Scottish accent. "Och, it's good tae be back."

"Well sit doon. Sit doon. I'll get you both some stew."

"You dinnae need to share with us," Eddard said. "We're fine."

"Nonsense," Maggie said, her eyes still closed. "Some MacGregors still share with guests no matter what that steward may do."

The meal was warm and good. Eddard stole glances at Jessica throughout. He found himself wondering if they would see another night together. Tomorrow, everything would change. One way or another it would all be over soon.

He wasn't sure whether to be glad or not.

Drummond yawned while they scraped the last of the food from their bowls. "We have little space but you can lay together by the fire if you like. It will stay warm a while longer yet."

"You dinnae want to stay up and play dice?" Eddard asked. "Like the old days?"

"No he does not," Maggie said, her eyes opening briefly. "He has little enough money to gamble with as it is."

"Good night," Drummond said, climbing into

the bed beside his wife. A minute later he was snoring loudly.

Jessica arranged the blankets by the fire, clambering into them and looking up at him. By the light of the flames she looked at her prettiest.

He climbed in beside her, lying back on the flattened earth below them. "Where are you from?" he whispered. "Your Scottish accent is no affectation. It is a natural one."

"I don't know where I'm from," she replied, her eyes half closed, her hands behind her head.

"Why not?"

"I was brought up in foster care, without my parents, I mean."

"Did they no tell you where you were from?"

"I asked but no one seemed to know. It was like I appeared from nowhere as far as they were concerned. I never understood it but I learned to live with it."

"You're from the Highlands, I would swear to it."

"Maybe I am. Who knows? Not that it matters."

"Where's home now then? Where do you want this key to send you?"

"Far from here."

"By tomorrow night we might both be dead. You might as well tell me."

She sighed, turning onto her side and looking at him. "Just a caveat. This is going to sound insane, okay?"

"Okay."

"I'm from the future."

"You're from the future?"

"Don't look at me like that."

"Like what?"

"Like I'm crazy. I swear, I've come back in time. I don't know why, I just know the key brought me here and I get the strangest feeling it did it for a reason. You don't believe me, do you?"

Eddard thought he'd kept the skepticism from his face but clearly not. "I believe you believe that's true."

"You sound like a politician. Look, I'll prove it to you."

"How?"

"When we get the key, I'll show you through the door to my time."

"Then we need not argue now, future lass."

"I know it sounds crazy, okay? If someone said it to me, I'd think they were crazy. I think I'm crazy but dreams don't last this long. This is real, isn't it? I'm really here?"

"Aye."

"What? Why are you looking like that?"

"Like what?"

She leaned closer. He could feel her breath on his face. "Like you're not really here. Like your mind's far away."

"I'm thinking about tomorrow."

"You don't think we can do this, do you? Convince them I'm Morag, I mean."

He was silent for a moment, taking a swig from the leather flask before speaking. "I was supposed to protect her. I was meant to be guarding the door the night she went missing. It's my fault all this happened, all the pain the clan is going through. It's all because of me."

"That was twenty years ago, wasn't it? How old were you then? Twelve? Fourteen? You were a child. It wasn't your fault what happened."

He shook his head, needing to get it all out. "I had to look after the horses. Ronald sent me because they were restless, made me deal with them without finding cover. He said it would only take me a couple of minutes.

"By the time I got back, she was gone and they were all talking about how I'd abandoned my post. No one believed me when I said Ronald had sent me away. For all I know he killed the lass and hid her body."

"She's not dead," a voice said in the dark. It was Maggie. They looked up at her but she was fast asleep, or appeared to be. "She's alive and closer than you think, Eddard MacGregor."

They waited but she didn't say anything else.

"That was weird," Jessica said, stifling a yawn.

"You must sleep," Eddard told her, lying down and throwing an arm over her, drawing her against him in the way they'd both become used to. It felt strange to think it would be their last night together.

"I don't want to sleep," she said quietly. "If I sleep tomorrow comes and after that all this is over."

"You mean you like sleeping on the dirt?"

"I mean…never mind."

She said nothing else. Soon her breathing became steady. It took a lot longer for Eddard to fall asleep and when he did he dreamed of the day the princess went missing.

He ran upstairs in the keep, hearing her calling his name. He reached the corridor and it wasn't the princess calling for help. It was Jessica. She was being pushed through a door by a figure in the shadows. She cried for him to stop but he couldn't run.

His limbs moved but in slow motion, like wading through a swamp, the floor at his feet gripping his boots. He tried to reach her. He strained every muscle in his body but just as his fingers brushed over hers, she vanished. The door slammed shut and the figure in the darkness muttered, "Too late."

He sat up in the cottage, sweat pouring down him despite the cold. The fire had long since died.

He shook his head. It was just a dream. It didn't mean anything.

He lay down once more, closing his eyes and praying he would dream no more that night. His prayers went unanswered. All night he spent running down the corridor, trying to save the princess over and over, save Jessica, save the princess, the two people blurring into one.

Beside him Jessica slept on, dreaming her own dreams of doors slamming in the dark, echoing sounds that bounced around her head until her ears rang from the noise.

Chapter Ten

J essica was back at MacGregor Castle. It was a surreal experience. She was probably the only person in the history of the world who could do a direct comparison between how it looked in the twenty-first century and the thirteenth.

The track leading to the main gate followed roughly the same route as in her time though pebbles and mud took the place of the asphalt she remembered.

Drummond had given them both hooded woollen cloaks to wear and they looked like monks, standing stock still on a hilltop near the castle.

Eddard stood next to her, deep in thought. She said nothing. They would move when he had decided the best approach. She had no suggestions to make. This was his world, not hers.

The men pacing back and forth in front of the gate had swords at their side, swords that would be sharp even if the blacksmith's work was poor.

Their armor glinted in the early morning light, their faces hidden behind helmets. How were they going to get in there?

While he mulled, she ran her eyes over the castle. From the hill where they stood they could see it clearly though they remained hidden by the surrounding trccs.

Eddard had mentioned them when they first left the cottage that morning. "In my time all vegetation was kept clear to give a clear line of sight for the archers. One more thing Ronald has neglected. See that crumbling wall? If that is not resolved by winter the entire east side of the battlements will come down like the abbey wall where I found you."

The gate she already knew. That was where she'd first approached the site. That patch of grass, that was the parking lot in her time. The walls looked pretty much the same apart from the crumbled section and its surrounding scaffolding.

It was odd seeing guards pacing the battlements below the pennants that fluttered in the light breeze.

Crows circled the great keep, their cawing the only sound.

She looked to her right when she heard a noise. Carts were approaching, laden with goods.

"They are about to open for the morning," Eddard said. "It's now or never. Do you recall what Angela taught you?"

"I am Morag MacGregor and my parents are Rachel and Cam. I have a little brother, Philip. I'm definitely not Jessica Abrahams."

"Dinnae forgo the accent."

"Och, jings, of course not. Cease your blether, you great pile o' haggis."

"All right, save it for when we get down there. You ready?"

"As I'll ever be. You're sure this will work?"

"Aye."

There was something he wasn't telling her. She could see it in his eyes. He had become colder since last night. Was it nerves? Or something else?

Perhaps it was simply remembering his part in the princess going missing. She wanted to tell him again that it wasn't his fault but they were already walking down the hillside toward the castle. The conversation would have to wait.

They fell in line with the carts, slowing their step

until they came to a stop while the guards questioned the first in line at the gate.

"What's in the cart?"

"Apples for selling. You want to buy, I'll give you a good price."

"Looks heavy for apples."

"It's just a good crop, that's all."

All at once he was being dragged away by one of the guards, pulled through the gate and into the castle. The other guard moved around the side of the cart and shoved two sacks onto the floor. Underneath were bottles filled with a dark liquid. "Smuggling wine," the guard shouted to his colleague. "Without paying the tax."

"I dinnae ken how that got on there," the man shouted back. "I'm innocent, I tell you."

The drama over, two laborers were called over to shift the cart inside. "Confiscated," the guard told them. "Belong to the steward now."

The laborers nodded and headed inside, guiding the donkey that pulled the cart. The guards were back in their places by the time Eddard and Jessica made it to the front of the queue. She tried to control her shaking hands but she could do nothing about her thudding heart. Was she breathing too fast? She felt like she was breathing too fast.

"State your business," the taller of the two guards said, holding out a hand to stop them entering.

"I bring something most valuable for the Laird and his Lady," Eddard said, keeping his head down, hidden under the hood.

"Oh, yes? And what that might be?"

"Their daughter."

The guard turned to Jessica, lifting her hood. "Wait here," he said, turning to talk quietly with his colleague. He vanished into the castle a moment later, closing the gate behind him, leaving the remaining guard to stare at Jessica.

She could only see his eyes through the slit of his helmet, they eyed her suspiciously. Was he one of the ones who dragged her to the steward when she was last here? Was this a mistake? Were they about to be killed before they even made it inside?

They didn't have to wait long. The gate opened and through it came the guard with a portly figure beside him. Jessica recognized his oily grin at once. "You," she said. "Give me back my key."

She lunged at him but the guard shoved her back. "Do not touch the Laird's steward."

"Key?" the steward asked, sounding surprised. "I dinnae ken anything about a key. You will turn and walk away from here if you value your life."

"No," Eddard said firmly. "We will not."

"And who is hiding under that hood? Who did you bring to protect you? Another liar?"

"I am no liar," Eddard said, pushing back his hood and standing upright, looking taller than ever. "We will see the Laird and you will not stop us."

"Kill them," the steward said, waving his hand lazily.

The guards were fast but Eddard was faster. From flicking up his cloak to thrusting his sword into the air took less than a second. As the guards attacked he countered with a twist of his arm, his sword absorbing their blows with seemingly no effort.

He pushed forward, knocking the two of them off balance. It was over in another second. As they stumbled he dropped his sword and slammed their heads together. They slumped to the ground and lay still. The steward's eyes widened in panic. "You cannae come in here." He held his ground though his hands were shaking.

"Try and stop us," Eddard said, punching him

on the chin and sending him spinning around on the spot before he fell to his knees.

"Come on." Eddard grabbed Jessica's hand and together they ran into the castle leaving the steward yelling for help from a prone position on the ground.

"I need the key from him," Jessica said, trying to twist free from Eddard's grip.

"That can wait. We need to get you to the Laird and Lady first. The guards will kill you if you tarry."

They ran across the courtyard as a bell began to ring. "In here," Eddard said, pushing open a door and shoving Jessica inside. He followed, bolting the door behind them.

"Where are we?"

She knew the answer before he said it. They were in the keep. She knew this part. It was where she'd been taken for the guided tour. Around the corner and up the stairs and there would be her parents' bedroom.

Wait.

Why did she think that?

It would be the Laird and Lady's bedroom. Not her parents. She had no idea who they were.

"Up here," Eddard said, checking the door

behind them was secure. "Before he gets reinforcements. God, that punch felt good. I've been waiting to give him that for a very long time." He'd reopened the cut in his hand but it was worth it.

They ascended the narrow stone stairs, walking out into a corridor little different from her time. There was the door. In front of it another guard stood. He looked their way when they appeared but said nothing.

"We must see the Laird," Eddard said to him. "It is most urgent."

"None may pass."

"They will want to hear what we have to tell them."

"Be on your way before I have you both thrown in the dungeon."

"Please," Jessica tried. "Will you just look at me. Who do you think I am?"

"Let me guess. Morag?"

There was a thump downstairs. "They're getting through," Eddard said. "We are running out of time."

"So you recognize me?" Jessica asked the guard who seemed utterly indifferent to the noise downstairs.

"There have been many claiming to be the

missing princess. Too many. They will see no more claimants. The pain is too great. Be off with you."

A crash downstairs. Feet running, voices shouting.

The door opened behind the guard. A pale ethereal figure in white appeared in the gloom within.

"My Lady," the guard said, bowing deeply. "I apologize for the disturbance. I was just dealing with-"

She held up a hand, silencing the guard at once. "I will speak with these people."

At the end of the corridor more guards appeared, the steward among them. "Two thieves," he said as he marched to the front and grabbed Jessica by the arm. "Go back inside, I will deal with them at once."

"You will do nothing of the sort," Rachel said. "You will all wait there. You-" she pointed at Jessica, "-will come with me."

Jessica gulped. Under the piercing eyes of the woman in front of her, she felt utterly exposed. She could not stop herself walking through the door, leaving the steward to stand with his mouth open, staring after her. She knew that woman. Where from?

As her eyes adjusted to the gloom she was able to make out the contents of the room. It was funny. She would have guessed its layout even without seeing it. Over there was another door to the garret.

From the garret she heard movement. A shadow fell across the floor and then disappeared. Someone was in there. The Laird?

"You ken me, do you not?" Rachel asked.

Out in the corridor the steward coughed, trying to get the Lady's attention.

Jessica tried not to wilt under the fierce onslaught of the Lady's eyes. "I know you're the Lady of Clan MacGregor, wife of Cam MacGregor, Laird of these people and the lands from the north down to the Dark River."

Where did those words come from? They were out of her mouth as if a rote response. What was happening?

Rachel nodded. "I came here with a key many years ago. My daughter, my true daughter, went missing years ago."

Jessica nodded, her heart pounding so hard in her chest she thought it might explode. Would they realise she was pretending to be their daughter?

Rachel continued. "I was told she would return with a key of her own. Do you have a key?"

"I did have one. The steward stole it from me."

"A lie," the steward said, coming in and grabbing hold of Jessica by the arm. "She is a thief and will be dealt with accordingly. Now come on, you have disturbed the peace of the castle long enough." He dragged her out of the room, shouting loudly. "This woman just assaulted the Lady. Take her to the dungeon."

Jessica looked back and saw Rachel in the doorway, looking mournful. "Help us," she shouted but the guards were pulling the doors closed. It was starting to look more like the Laird and Lady were prisoners in their own castle. What she needed was to get them alone, away from the steward.

That was easier said than done as she was dragged down the stairs and into the bowels of the castle.

She could see Eddard trying to fight them off. At first it looked as if he'd win but there were just too many of them and too little space. Soon he was as helpless as her and that was when she felt truly lost for the first time since she'd met him.

At the bottom of another staircase she was shoved through a doorway. Before she had time to react it was slammed shut, a key rattling on the other side. She thought for a moment she might have been sent back home but no, it was a dark and dank prison cell.

"She is to be executed," the steward said to someone on the other side. "Tried to murder the Laird and Lady." The voice faded away and then she was alone in a deafening silence.

The room was lit only by a thin window high above her head. A thin strip of light hit the far wall, barely enough to illuminate the interior of the cell. Where was Eddard? Was he imprisoned nearby?

Fear rose within her as she thought about what the steward had said. Executed? She prayed this was a dream, one from which might she might wake up at any moment.

A jangle of chains made her jump and then she noticed someone in the corner, sitting cross legged and plaiting lengths of straw together.

She crossed the cell and sat down opposite the figure. It was a woman a similar age to herself, red hair lank and falling over her shoulders. Her skin was bruised. "How long have you been in here?" she asked.

The woman looked up at her. "A week."

"What for?"

The woman smiled. "Has he sent you here to get me to talk?"

"Who?"

"Ronald. The pig who walks on two legs."

"Did he put you in here?"

"Aye and to think he used to pay me for my services. Told me I would be his Lady when he became Laird."

"What? How did you end up in here, then?"

The woman set down the ends of straw and stretched her hands out in front of her. "I ken something he shared that he regrets sharing."

"What's that?"

"The clan is ruined. He's been siphoning money for himself for years and spending it all. He even borrowed from the moneylenders and owes so much the whole place will be ruined by the end of the month."

"So that's why he plans to rob the tax train then," Jessica said more to herself than to her fellow prisoner. "It's funny. I never knew that word was so old."

"Huh?"

"Never mind. Just talking to myself. Why are you looking like that? There's something else isn't there?"

"He's been doping the Laird and Lady. It was the only way he could get them to stay in hiding.

He's going to blame the Laird for the crime, go tell the King that Cam stole it all."

"Why do that?"

"Because then Cam gets his head cut off for the crime and Ronald can claim the Lairdship for himself. It's funny, I never thought he'd have the brains to come up with something like that. He never seemed that smart."

"And he put you in here to stop you talking?"

"Aye but I reckon he's forgotten about me. He said I'd be dead by the next day and yet here I am, surviving on the mice and rainwater."

"We need to get out of here, tell the Laird and Lady of his scheme before it's too late."

"We are locked in a dungeon, lass. There is no escape until the door is unlocked."

"I'm a private investigator. I've been locked in quite a few places in my time. Just give me a minute to think."

She got up and walked around the room, examining it in detail before turning back to her companion. "I have an idea."

Chapter Eleven

E ddard sat cross legged on the floor of the cell, preserving his energy. He had no idea how long he might be down there or how often food might be provided, if at all.

The steward had spoken of execution and he knew exactly what that entailed. He had seen a hanging once before his exile. He remembered nothing of the crime committed, only that it must have been very serious.

The condemned man stood at the top of the steps, his hands bound behind his back, his eyes wild with fear as he begged for someone, anyone in the crowd to help him, to save him from what was going to happen.

Eddard stood with all the others. He didn't want

to but his father had made him. What he remembered was the trembling of the prisoner's legs as he was walked to the spot. He was lifted onto the stool, his legs bound.

"It's so he can't kick," Eddard's father told him. "Sometimes they struggle." The noose was wrapped around the man's neck as he continued to plead for mercy.

The priest intoned a loud prayer for the soul of the condemned and then the sight Eddard could remember as if it were yesterday, even though the man's name had long left his memory.

The stool was kicked away and in that moment the man locked eyes with Eddard. It was for the briefest of instants before the rope went taut but it was long enough.

In that look Eddard saw only abject terror, the like of which he had never seen before or since.

In the cell of MacGregor Castle he had time to think of that man. Had he been held in the same cell? Perhaps pacing back and forth? Perhaps muttering prayers or curses to himself as he waited.

Eddard was silent. If execution was to be his end he would accept it. What he would not accept, what he would never accept, was the execution of Jessica. She had committed no crime. She had done not a thing wrong since she arrived in his life. All she wanted was to go home.

He had brought her here, he had lied that she was the Laird and Lady's daughter, he had used her to get back into the castle. He had put her in danger.

The thought pained him far more than any fear of execution or torture. She was only at risk because of him. Her life would have been infinitely better if she had never met him.

He cursed his own idiocy. How could he have been so stupid? To have thought he could simply wander back into the castle after all these years and pick things up where he left them, get rid of the man no one else could, as if he were savior of the clan. He was an arrogant fool and perhaps he deserved his fate.

His fists clenched without him realizing. He pushed them into the rotten straw underneath him, ignoring the smell, ignorant of the feel of decades of filth under his fingers. An anger rose in him, a righteous anger that he would do at least one good thing before his end.

No matter how many came for him, no matter how soon, or how slow. He would save her. He had no idea how he would do it but that mattered not.

He would rescue her and get her home, away from all this danger.

Maybe she was from the future. Maybe the key would work. He would leave that to fate. What he could control, he would. For now that meant controlling his temper and conserving his energy.

He tried not to think about how close they had come to succeeding. When he had punched Ronald on the jaw, he should have knocked him out, not rushed past into the castle.

He couldn't risk killing him. Do that and the guards would hold him for murder before he could reach the Laird's chamber. He should have done more. He should have planned better.

Stop.

He made himself concentrate on his breathing. That way he would be calm and ready. At some point the door to the cell would open. Guards would come in and try to remove him.

He was already working through the moves he would use to take them out. They had taken him by surprise in the keep. It would not happen again. Whoever came through that door next would not see daylight again. He swore to it.

Time passed.

He had no way of telling how long. Twice he

stood and paced around the cell, ensuring his legs were exercised. Other than that, he only sat and waited and tried his best not to think.

To think invited thoughts of her, of that beguiling look she got in her eyes when she talked to him, of the way her body felt when he held her at night. He would save her. Nothing would stop him.

A scrape on the other side of the door and he was instantly alert. He retreated into the shadows in the furthest recesses of the stinking cell. There was no light, only darkness.

He needed to be ready in case a torch was thrust in, the light could be enough to distract him if he was not prepared. To go from pitch black to bright flame would favor the guards over him.

A key thudded home into the lock. He flexed his fingers, taking a deep breath. He rolled back onto his heels, bending his knees slightly, ready to spring.

The door opened and he pounced at the sight of the lit candle thrust inside. By the time the guard was inside he was on him. He had his hands around the man's neck before he realized who it was.

"Stop," the figure gasped. "Stop!" The candle fell to the floor but kept burning.

Eddard knocked his opponent's hood from his head and gasped. "Jessica?" He let go of her neck, stepping back from her, afraid of his own strength. He had almost killed her. "I'm so sorry."

"Is that how you greet all your friends?" she said, her voice hoarse as she collapsed into a fit of coughs.

"I thought you were one of the guards. What are you doing here?"

"I've come to rescue you. I didn't expect to get throttled for my trouble."

He shook his head, grabbing both her cheeks and planting a rough kiss on her lips. "I can't believe you're here. Did they let you out?"

She shook her head. "I escaped." She looked slightly dazed.

"You escaped the dungeon of MacGregor Castle? Impossible."

"Then I guess I'm not really here and you didn't really just kiss me and then act like nothing happened. Maybe you're hallucinating."

Voices echoed down to them from the floor above. "This way," Eddard whispered. "We must be cautious."

He took her hand and together they edged out of the cell, ascending the stairs as quietly as they could manage. The voices faded away.

"A patrol," Eddard whispered in her ear. "They

will notice our absence soon enough. We must get to the Laird and Lady and prove to them you are Morag before our escape is noticed."

They passed along a narrow corridor and then another before pausing as more voices reached them. "In here," Jessica said, pulling open a door and slipping through it.

Eddard joined her just in time, the voices turning a corner and walking past the closet where they'd squeezed themselves. They stopped outside and Eddard held his breath, ready to attack if they should open the door.

"Well, where has he gone?" one of the figures outside was saying.

"Rumor has it that he's locked the Laird and Lady in their chamber while he goes off to do it."

"To do what? Everyone's talking about this thing he's doing. Most of the guards are gone. How are the two of us supposed to patrol the entire place. What if we're attacked while he's away?"

"No one kens the guards have gone with him. We look like guards don't we? We're wearing guard uniform."

"We look like kitchen boys in guard uniform."

"That's because we are kitchen boys in guard uniform. Now can we get moving?"

The door cracked open an inch on its hinge. Eddard went to grab the handle but it widened no further. Through the gap he could see the two of them out there.

One was tall and barely fit into the armor, the chainmail stretched across his chest so far it looked like it might burst into a thousand pieces at any moment. The shorter skinny one was holding a leather flask. He had no helmet on and his face was marked by the pox.

"I'm going nowhere until I finish this drink."

"Good grief, this is why you're not a guard. They wouldnae be seen dead drinking on duty. Serious offense, that is."

"Aye, and that's why I thought we best guard this corridor of the keep where none can see us who might tell Ronald. Now do you want some or not?"

"And if he asks what we were doing when he gets back?" asked the taller one, taking the flask and swigging from it. He belched loudly a second later.

"We say we went to check on the prisoners. He was laughing about them while he was being dressed ready for riding."

"Who do you think they were that he dragged down there?"

"No idea and I dinnae care. What I care about

is where he's gone with half the castle, most of the armory and all the stables."

"There is one horse left."

Eddard gave Jessica a look before peering out again. The two men were moving away, their voices fading. "He's gone to take the tax train on." The voice getting fainter. "So I hear tell anyway."

"But that passes by no more than an hour from here. They'll ken it's MacGregors that did it. We're all doomed."

"He's dressed them up in MacDonald colors, had the seamstresses making the baldrics for a month now. That's how I found out. Moira told me."

"You and her still a thing then?"

The men were gone, their voices too far away to be heard any longer.

Eddard pushed the door open and stepped out.

"That's what I was going to tell you," Jessica said. "What is a tax train anyway?"

"The king's accountants bring the taxes with them when they travel. As they move across the Highlands they gather his revenue and once all is collected they return to him for the funds to be added to the Royal coffers."

"So the taxes for all the clans is…?"

"On the back of their horses in wooden chests."

"And Ronald is going to steal it?"

"To be so brazen he must be desperate. If he doesn't succeed, the King will wipe Clan MacGregor from the face of the earth. If he succeeds, he'll have enough money to take over the Highlands in one fell swoop. He could hire an army bigger than the King's for the amount he'll bring back."

Jessica ran a hand through her hair. "What do we do?"

Eddard ran over to the nearest window and looked out. The sun was high in the sky. "It's noon. The tax train follows a schedule. It will pass through our territory not long after. The only place he could mount an assault is the deep pass between Mount Black and Mount Dalma. He will be there. If…" He lapsed into silence.

"If what?"

"I could get around the west side and warn the King in time. There is a ledge that few ken about and even fewer could traverse without falling."

"Then we must go at once."

He shook his head. "You should stay here where it's safe."

"You mean the place that put me in a dungeon and will do so again if I am caught?"

"You must make the Laird and Lady believe you are their daughter."

"You heard those guys. The Laird is locked away with his wife and who knows where. I'm coming with you."

"It will not be any pleasure voyage. I will ride hard and swift and the goat track around the mountain is-"

"Dangerous, I get it. I'm still coming with you."

"You are a stubborn lass."

"Get used to it. Now are we going or not?"

Eddard tried one last time. "We may not return alive."

"That," she said, slipping her hands into his while looking up into his eyes, "Is a risk worth taking."

Chapter Twelve

J essica thought she'd grown used to riding a horse but this was going to be something new. She could see from the moment the two of them entered the stable why this particular beast had been left behind.

"He's a destrier," Eddard said as Jessica stopped in the doorway. "A warhorse."

"He's not a horse, he's Godzilla," she replied, feeling the ground underneath her shake as the beast stamped its feet in the far stall, flicking its head violently as if daring them to get any closer. "You can't be expecting us to ride that."

"Och, he just needs the right touch, that's all."

Another violent stamp of its feet followed by baring its teeth at them, eyes bulging.

"I see the problem," Eddard said, taking a firm step forward. "Wait there."

"Wouldn't dream of moving," she replied, watching him make his way over to the stall. "Be careful." She had a sudden vision of him being picked up and tossed through the air the moment he got close enough.

It seemed impossible that horses could be that big. She remembered reading about destriers somewhere. Huge beasts that cost as much as a Laird might earn in a year.

They were bred to be fierce, trained never to show fear during battle. She had absolutely no doubt it would throw them both if they eventually managed to get on its back.

"Shush," Eddard said, hands held out toward the horse. "I ken you. You're Apollo, aren't you?" He glanced back at Jessica. "He was just a foal when I was last here and fierce enough then, took out the knee of the head groom. He was never the same after that."

"The horse or the groom?"

He smiled at her.

"Don't look at me, look at him."

He pulled open the stall door as the horse eyed him suspiciously, then the two of them were gone from sight. She waited a minute but after hearing nothing, edged her way over and peered inside. She could see at once what was happening.

The horse had its rear right hock bound with rope to an iron loop on the wall behind it. Eddard was busy undoing the knots which held it in place.

She was certain he'd be kicked at any moment but as the last of the rope fell away the horse calmed at once, turning and nudging his ear with its huge head.

"All right you great lummox," Eddard said, patting its neck. "Are we happier now?"

He led the horse out of the stall while Jessica marveled at his skill. The terrifying beast had become putty in Eddard's hands. She knew how it felt. His hands on her were enough to melt any anger she felt, no wonder he was having the same calming influence on the destrier.

In a couple of minutes the saddle was in place and it was like the furious animal had never been there. The huge beast placidly walked out into the courtyard mild as a lamb. "What if we're seen?" Jessica asked, glancing around her.

"What, by them two?" He nodded toward the courtyard steps. The two kitchen boys in guard uniform were asleep on their feet, slumped against each other. "Whatever they were drinking was strong stuff."

"Are you sure it won't hurt us?" she asked, looking up at the horse which stared straight ahead.

"I promise," he replied, taking her waist in his hands and lifting her effortlessly onto the back of the beast. She tried to think about balancing, not about the feel of his hands on her a moment earlier, the tingle that remained long after he'd let go.

He jumped on behind her and they set off toward the gate. "Open up," Eddard shouted to the porter sitting by his winch. "We have most urgent business on behalf of the steward."

The man had the gate open before he had time to stop and think. By the time he called them to stop they were already out and riding hard.

Eddard had one hand on her stomach, his arm pressing into her side, holding her firmly in place. The other hand was on the rein, guiding, not forcing the horse onward. The pace was tremendous. They thundered down the track, the horse breathing as heavily as her.

She was jolted back and forth in place and if it wasn't for Eddard, she would have fallen many times. Each corner sent her sliding off to the side and on those occasions he pulled her against his chest. How was he breathing so calmly? How was he not as worried as her?

Her thighs burned from gripping the side of the horse, her hands holding Eddard's arm. His muscles bulged and flexed until he seemed as brutish as the horse, the two beasts working together to reach the foot of the mountain faster than she ever thought possible.

"See that gap over there," Eddard shouted in her ear over the sound of the hooves. "That's where the steward is."

"How can you tell? I see nothing."

"The dust cloud, it rises from his horses. We have time but not much. He will soon be slowed by the steepness of a dozen crags he must top. We have an easier journey but soon we must continue on foot."

The horse didn't stop for another ten minutes and when it did, Jessica had to be helped down. Her legs had turned to jelly. "We have no time to waste," Eddard said, pushing her onto her back and massaging her thighs in his enormous hands, his fingers rubbing the cramps and spasms from her body.

She lay back and looked up at him, trying to work out what was going on in his head. Did he know he'd touched her more today than anyone ever before? Was it possible that the kiss he'd given her meant more than it had seemed at the time?

She found herself thinking about the kiss again. It obviously meant little to him yet why had he done it? She had no answer. She wanted it to mean something but she dared not hope too much. To hope was to invite disappointment especially as she would be going home soon. There was no point becoming attached to him.

"Better?" he asked, helping her to her feet.

"Much."

"You have strong legs. The best of riders could have lasted half that length of time on Apollo. You did well."

"Thanks," she said, unable to resist smiling. "I never knew I could ride."

"Can you climb though?"

"Climb? I thought you said it was a goat track we were following."

"Aye but we must get up to it." He pointed and she looked.

She felt her blood run cold. "We're climbing that?"

Where he'd pointed was a vertical cliff face. They were standing near the bottom of it and far above she could see tufts of grass hanging over the edge. Otherwise it was nothing but rock. She gulped as he tapped the horse on its flank. "Back home with you," he said. "You've done good."

The horse ignored him, crossing over to a stream on their left and taking a long drink.

"Stubborn," Eddard said with a smile. "I like him."

"Can we get back to the point in hand?" she asked, looking up at the cliff again. "I cannot climb that."

"You dinnae have to."

"You expect me to wait here for you to come back?"

"Nope." He turned and tapped his shoulder. "Hop on."

"What? You're going to piggyback me? You're crazy."

"We used to train here with full barrels strapped on our back as kids. You're half the weight and much softer than ash."

"If you drop me…" She couldn't think how to end the sentence but given her limited choices, she jumped onto his back, arms around his neck.

"Dinnae throttle me," he said, gasping slightly.

"Sorry," she said, loosening her grip.

"You must haud on tight. I must have my hands free to climb." He was already starting up the cliff as he spoke and by the time she thought to say this was a bad idea they were already twenty feet up.

She made the mistake of looking down. Their horse was already shrinking, looking more like a Shetland rather than a destrier. She closed her eyes, trying not to think what would happen if she fell.

"Count to ten," he said. "Out loud."

She did as he asked, each number matching a movement of his hands. He was gripping the smoothest of rock as if he were a spider climbing a wall, not a human. She had reached the number eight when he stopped moving.

"You can let go now," he said.

She opened her eyes. They had reached the goat track. "Oh," she said, glancing over the edge and almost falling as a wave of dizziness struck her. He grabbed her and held her tightly.

"You all right, lass?"

"I'll be fine," she replied, her dizziness easing as she stared into his eyes. She felt sure he would kiss her again but she was to be disappointed.

"This way," he said, letting go of her and starting to walk along the track.

If she ignored the height they were at, it wasn't

that difficult a journey. The goats had stamped down on the vegetation, creating a flattened path with an overhang in places where the rocks jutted out from the mountainside.

Here and there they had to duck, Eddard more often than her. On a couple of occasions they were reduced to crawling on hands and knees but as long as she ignored the cold wind and didn't look down, it was simple enough to make progress.

It was when she looked down that dizziness threatened to engulf her. Each time she did what he'd told her to do during the climb. She counted. By the time she reached ten, it passed.

She had no idea how long they traveled for, the path seeming to go forever.

Eventually, it began to slope downward. In the distance she could see a silver ribbon weaving its way toward the mountain. "That is the track we seek," Eddard said as if reading her mind. "See by that forest?"

She looked and there was a dust plume similar to the one they'd seen on their approach to the mountain range. "The tax train?" she asked.

"Aye, we are not too late. Come on, we can speed up now the ground is approaching."

Ten minutes later they were off the goat track

and marching as fast as they could through soft clumps of heather until they reached the track. Eddard looked left then right. "We shall wait here," he said. "They will be with us once they round that corner ahead. "It will not take long."

"What are you going to tell them?"

"The truth."

They waited. Jessica took the time to lay back in the heather that grew so profusely next to the track. She looked up at the sky and tried to slow her pounding heart. It felt as if she'd been on edge for days, without a chance to relax.

That wasn't true. She had felt relaxed each night, held in his arms, warmed by his skin. She felt a tingle inside her as she had when he'd kissed her. She was going to miss this place. Despite the danger, despite the cruelty, she would miss it.

She would miss the peace of moments like this, being able to lay next to a road without traffic roaring by. She would miss the sights and smells and most of all she would miss the Highlander who was motioning for her to sit up at that very moment. She couldn't stay even if she wanted to. Caroline needed her.

"Here they come," he said as the noise of horses grew louder. "Be ready."

Chapter Thirteen

E ddard made sure Jessica couldn't be seen. From his position in the middle of the road all he could see was heather and long grass. That way there was no risk of her getting a stray arrow to the face. He'd already warned her that if this failed, she should make her own way back to the island. There, Angela would know what to do next.

He waited as the first of the horses came into view. Destriers all of them, as tall as the one he'd taken from the stable, better armed though, their bodies covered in mail. Atop them were tall soldiers, the best trained the King could spare.

Behind the first four horses came the chests, hanging from the sides of the beasts, each one heavy with gold and silver. The movement of the train was slow, the weight of the taxes dictating the pace.

They saw him a moment later. Two of the men thundered toward him, leaving the rest to maintain their steady pace.

He was ready. As they approached, he held up his sword and then lay it on the ground in front of him, taking a step backward. "I mean no harm," he shouted over the sound of their thundering hooves.

"Make way for the King's men," the nearest soldier shouted. "You can be hanged for less than this."

"I must speak with your leader at once."

"You must do nothing."

The other soldier waved the first into silence. "Who are you?" he asked, raising his visor and looking down at Eddard.

"I am Eddard of the Clan MacGregor and I have news of a plot most foul."

The man looked at Eddard and then back at the rest of the train which had caught up with him. He held up a hand and the horses came to a halt. "You have honest eyes," the soldier said. "What is this plot of which you speak?"

"Ronald, steward of the MacGregors, awaits

you in the mountain pass ahead. He wears MacDonald colours and plans to slaughter you all and take those chests back to the castle with him."

"Does he indeed?"

"Why should we believe you?" someone shouted from further back. "You could be part of the plot."

The nearest soldier yelled, "Silence," before turning his attention back to Eddard. "Why are you telling us this?"

"Because I cannot stand by and let that man destroy the clan's reputation."

"The King will burn more than your reputation if he were to find out you're lying. Come, you will walk with us. If you speak the truth one more sword will be useful. If you are lying, yours will be the first head to roll."

Eddard stepped forward and retrieved his sword. He caught a glimpse of Jessica out the corner of his eye and motioned for her to stay hidden. One way or another, it was better she was not involved in the upcoming battle.

The train began to move and he went with them, his long strides helping him keep pace with the horses. As the path grew steeper the progress slowed.

"It is a good place for an ambush," the man

nearest him said. "My name is Forbes MacCallister by the way."

"The King's personal guard?"

"The same. Rumor was that we would encounter some trouble this time."

Eddard nodded. For the King's personal guard to be away from him was rare. "You heard of the plan?"

"No, but we heard whispers that your steward is up to something. News travels fast even this far north. Why would he do something as foolish as take on the King's men? He must ken he will be found out."

"He planned to blame the Laird and take over the clan himself."

"Assault and then take credit for finding the culprits. A smart move. Shame it will be his last. Where will he be?"

"Around that bend there is a series of boulders either side of the pass. He will have positioned his men behind them, I have no doubt. They are tall enough to hide them and you must pass through the gap one at a time as it narrows. He can shut off your retreat and your advance."

"Like fish in a barrel," Forbes replied. "But we

shall fool him yet. Jock, Art, leave your horses and see if our friend here speaks the truth."

The train paused again as two men scrambled up the sheer mountain side like strolling through rolling pasture. They soon vanished from sight.

"If what you say is right, you will be rewarded most handsomely," Forbes said while they waited. "What would you have? Land? Money? Women?

"I want only that which you cannot give," he replied.

"Tis a woman then." Forbes laughed. "Dinnae look so surprised. It is always a woman."

The two men reappeared, giving a nod to Forbes who turned to Eddard. "Get your sword out lad, you'll need it." He turned to the others. "Four men each side of the pass. Use your horses to run them down as they approach. Eddard here will draw them to us. Think you can do it?"

Eddard nodded as the other men prepared. He walked past them, feeling the coldness pass over him that he knew so well from his training. It had never left him.

He turned the corner and was alone, like he was the only person in the country. There was no noise from in front or behind. Either side of him the mountains rose up, keeping the pass in shadow. There were the boulders.

He walked forward, sword drawn, stopping about ten feet from the nearest boulder. "Ronald," he shouted at the top of his voice. "Come out and fight like a man."

A man emerged a second later, a man Eddard didn't recognize. He was bald and wearing a monk's cowl. "What are you doing here?" the man asked. "This does not concern you."

"Then kill me."

The man smiled. "Very well." He whistled and half a dozen knights emerged. Eddard let them approach, waiting for the right moment. When they were five feet away, he turned tail and fled, sprinting back to the corner.

He could hear the steward calling behind him. "Coward. Real men dinnae run from a fight."

He turned the corner and almost skidded into the end of an outstretched sword. Forbes took one look at him, nodded, and then urged his horse forward.

Eddard spun on his feet in time to see the half dozen knights who'd been chasing him get run down by the destriers. He made it around the corner in time to see the battle almost over.

Men were dying, swords clashing loudly, screams echoing around the pass. In the distance he could see Ronald on his horse, sprinting away from the scene. "Real men dinnae run from a fight," he yelled after him as an unmanned horse stumbled toward him.

He grabbed it, flinging himself on top, ready to ride after the steward.

"Not without me," a voice called out.

He looked back and there was Jessica running toward him. "Hurry," he shouted. "He's getting away."

She grabbed his hand and was on a second later. Galloping past the battle, they rode hard but the steward was already far ahead.

He glanced behind him, gratified to find only the King's men remained standing. The dying were either the steward's men or hired fighters.

It was probably for the best that they had been slaughtered. The clan could begin anew with fresh guards who were not beholden to that villain who was trying his best to outride them.

By the time they made it to MacGregor Castle, the steward was already there, rallying what few men he could find around him. There were kitchen boys, grooms, even the gong scourer had been roped into guarding the main gate.

Eddard didn't slow, riding straight at them. They scattered at once and then he was in the courtyard with nothing between him and the steward.

"Kill him!" Ronald screamed.

Eddard said nothing. He marched over and swung his fist, catching the steward on the jaw and sending him flying. His head bounced off the wall beside him and he slumped down to the ground, his cry of pain cut off. Eddard lifted his head as Jessica ran over.

"Dead?" she asked.

"Just knocked out," he replied, noticing the chain around the steward's neck. "I believe this is yours." He yanked and the chain snapped. On the end was the key just as Jessica had described to him.

"Eddard MacGregor," a voice boomed out.

He looked up and there were the Laird and Lady on the steps of the keep. The men around him bowed down and he did the same. "My Laird."

The Lady was already descending, making not for him but for Jessica.

The Laird continued to shout. "Tell me why I

should not have you hanged for attacking my loyal steward?"

"Your loyal steward just tried to rob the King of his taxes and he planned to blame you for the crime so he could take over the clan. How's that for a reason?"

The Laird looked shocked. "Ronald would never do that."

"Forbes will be here soon enough. You can ask him if I speak the truth."

The Laird wasn't looking at him anymore. He was looking at Jessica. The Lady had reached her and was examining her closely.

"You have her eyes," Rachel said. "Tell me, may I see your arm?"

Jessica pulled up her sleeve to expose her skin to the Lady and her husband.

"You have the scar," Rachel said, running her finger along it. "You have the key and the scar. You are Morag."

"What?" Jessica said. "You believe that?"

"Where were you born?"

"Here at the castle," she replied without pausing.

"Where have you been?"

"The steward," she said, blinking as if she was

just waking up. "The steward used the key to send me away."

"Where to?"

"Far away."

She began to cry and the Laird and Lady embraced her. Eddard shook his head. This was the time to do it, not focus on them.

While they were distracted he made his way to the treasury. Somehow he was not surprised to find barely a copper coin inside. The cupboard was bare.

He made his way back out to an empty courtyard. The door to the brewery was open and his feet took him inside. He had achieved his goal.

In a way.

It felt like a hollow victory though. The first chance Jessica would get, she'd use the key to go home and he'd be left to explain to the Laird why he'd conned them.

The scar. What about the scar?

He had no answer to that other than coincidence. Inside the brewery was a long table, the nearest the castle came to a tavern. Only one other person was in there. A woman who had been beaten recently.

"Good day," the woman said, raising a tankard as he entered. "Seeking business?"

"Not with you," he replied before she had a chance to show her wares. There was only one woman he wanted and it was not a tipsy witch trying to sell potions of nonsense.

"Last person to use my stuff stole them and stole me. Why not pour yourself a drink and we'll sit in despair together?"

He did so, taking a seat and draining half his tankard in one go.

"It could be worse," the woman said. "I was in a cell yesterday and now look at me. If I get drunk enough, maybe I willnae mind seeing Ronald's face no more."

"I think he'll be leaving fairly soon," Eddard said.

The door to the brewery hit the wall with a bang. Eddard turned and there was the steward, his eyes wild.

"What are you doing here?" Ronald asked, staring at the woman. "What have you told him?"

"What? About you poisoning the Laird and Lady with herbs stolen from me, addling their brains so they let you send Philip away? They've had years in hiding because of you dripping poison into their food and into their ears. I am no longer afraid of you."

Ronald smiled. "You should be. So now the exile kens the truth?" He spat onto the floor. "Shame neither of you will get to tell anyone else. Time to kill you both." He began swinging a sword in front of him, cutting through the air with menace. "Who wants to die first?"

"Neither of them," a voice said from the doorway behind him.

The steward froze as the Laird walked inside.

"What are you doing, Ronald?"

"Why are you out, my Laird? You should be in the chapel praying for your daughter's safe return."

"We will eat nothing more that you provide. You will not control our behaviour anymore. Guards!"

Four men ran in, grabbing hold of the steward as he protested in words that fell between curses and blasphemy. "You'll all pay for this," he said as he was dragged outside.

The Laird walked across to Eddard and held out a hand. "I am in your debt."

Eddard shook, not sure what to say.

"I feel immense shame at what my steward has done in my name. Philip will return home at once.

Morag is where she belongs and I feel as if I am awake for the first time in years. Accept my apologies for your exile. Whatever you wish for, name it and it shall be your reward."

"I want only one thing and it is something you cannot give."

The Laird frowned and then smiled. "I think I understand. Wait here a moment."

Chapter Fourteen

✿

When Jessica was twelve, she was hit by a car. It gave her a glancing blow before skidding to a halt, the elderly driver running over and apologizing profusely. "I thought I hit the brake," she said as if that explained everything.

How she felt just before the car hit was how she felt when Rachel touched the scar on her arm, the one she knew nothing about where it had come from.

There was a heavy feeling in her feet and in the pit of her stomach, as if she wanted to move but was glued to the spot. A tidal wave washed over her, leaving her unable to breathe. Her only thought was white. A white light that filled her eyes and her mind, wiping away the present and sending her back in time.

As she stood in the courtyard saying words without even knowing where they were coming from, more and more memories came to her, each one flashing by before she had a chance to process them.

They embraced her but she felt nothing. What was happening to her? Was this something to do with the time travel? What would happen when they found out the truth? That she wasn't their daughter?

Before she knew it she was inside the keep with the Laird and Lady. The three of them were alone. The Lady took her hand and together they stood by the fireplace. On the mantelpiece above it was a doll. A doll she recognized.

"I left my babby lying here,

Lying here, lying here.

I left my babby lying here.

Tae go and gather blaeberries."

Jessica looked into the eyes of the woman in front of her, seeing them rimmed with tears. "I know that song," she said, staggering back as a memory hit her that was so powerful she blacked out.

She was a child, walking along a corridor, leaving her parents behind. She lived in the castle. She'd always lived in the castle. She'd been born in the castle. She had a brother. He was a baby.

The lullaby was running through her head as she passed through a door to retrieve her doll. The key turning. The key in the door. That was it.

She opened her eyes and looked up into the worried face of the Lady above her. "Mom?" she asked, sitting up slowly. "Is that you?"

"Morag," Rachel said, openly weeping as she drew her daughter into her arms.

"Mom," Jessica said.

She wasn't Jessica. That was the name they'd given her when they found her alone and scared in the twenty-first century. She was Morag. Her name was Morag. She almost passed out again, her head throbbing with memories as if it had been asleep for years and was just waking up for the first time.

She hugged her mother and this time she felt more emotions than she could handle. Her eyes closed as she began to cry, her mother continuing to sing the lullaby to her, her father nowhere to be seen.

"Where have you been all this time?" Rachel asked a little later. The two of them were sitting in the Laird's private quarters, their faces red from the tears. Outside crows were cawing loudly but inside there was little noise.

Morag thought how to answer, the silence in the room feeling heavy. She was still trying to piece together the snippets of memories that rolled around inside her head. "You wouldn't believe me if I told you."

"Try me," Rachel replied, turning the little silver key over in her hands. "I never thought I'd see a key like this again."

"You recognize it?"

"You first. Where have you been all this time?"

"The future." She winced, expecting disbelief or confusion. Instead, Rachel smiled. "You were in the twenty-first century, right?"

"How did you know that?"

"I'm from that time. A key brought me back here long before you were born, before I even met your father."

"You mean you're from the future?"

"I'm guessing it was the bond between us that sent you there. But how did you get back?"

Jessica told her all she could remember. She began explaining about the day she went missing. "It was the steward," she said suddenly. "That's where I knew him from. I knew I'd seen him somewhere. He locked me in the linen closet upstairs with that key."

With that revelation she continued, leaving in the gaps that remained in her memory. When she said how the key came to her, Rachel smiled.

"Someone out there is watching over our family. I was sent a key too, in a manner of speaking."

"But who sent it to me?"

"I doubt we'll ever know the answer to that. So the key brought you back here, did it?"

"It did, only when I arrived the steward stole it and I ended up on Kirrin Island."

She quickly summed up what had happened since, her meeting up with Eddard, their journey back to the castle together. The chase after the steward to prevent him stealing from the tax train.

"He's clearly a good man," Rachel said. "You chose your traveling companion well. Yet you look forlorn. You are wondering if you can leave him and return to the future, aren't you?"

Morag sat up in her chair. "How did you guess?"

"I felt the same, although I was not born in this time as you were. Time is a strange thing, not that people ever really think about it that much. Read a book and you travel through space and time and no one bats an eyelid. Us?

"We really have traveled through time and you have my sympathy as you belong to two times far more than I ever did. My heart always lay here with Cam and his people. You should stay here and be with Eddard."

"How do you-?"

"Know how you feel about him? Call it a mother's intuition."

"Look, even if I wanted to stay here, I can't."

"Why not?"

Getting up, Morag crossed to the window and looked out at the countryside beyond the castle walls. "There's a girl I promised to look after. Caroline. I can't just abandon her."

"Who is she?" Rachel asked, coming to join her by the window.

"She lived in the apartment block. Her parents beat her up. She kept asking me to take care of her but I couldn't do much. I can't leave her to that life."

"You might not have to. Come over here."

Rachel walked over to the door and pulled it closed.

"What are you doing?"

"Watch." She slid the silver key into the lock and turned it. When she opened the door again the corridor outside had gone. Instead it was like looking out from Morag's old apartment. There were the stairs leading down. There the worn carpet and there sitting alone was Caroline, weeping silently.

"Caroline," Morag said, walking out through the door and across to her. "What's wrong."

"They left a note," Caroline replied without looking up. "Said they didn't want me anymore. Told me to hand myself into the police."

She looked up, her face bruised and puffy. Morag crouched beside her. "There's an alternative to that."

"You said you couldn't be my mom."

"Maybe I changed my mind." She held out a hand and Caroline took it. "Come on," she added. "I've got something to show you. Just don't freak out, okay?"

She walked through the door and as she did so, Rachel stepped back, watching them both in silence. "Is this your apartment?" Caroline asked, looking around the room with her eyes wide. "It looks so old."

"It's the Middle Ages," Rachel said. "And you're welcome to stay if you want."

"That's my Mom," Morag added. "Look back through that door."

Caroline did, seeing the corridor of the apartment block.

"You can walk back through there and stay there if you want or you can come and live here with me but-"

"With you," Caroline said, pushing the door closed. It opened a second later, the Laird walking in. Outside, here was only the corridor of the castle in view. "Where did it go? What happened?"

"It's gone," Rachel said. "The key has done its job."

The Laird looked at Caroline in surprise, taking in her clothes and her face before turning to Morag. "I think you should go and talk to Eddard. He's in the courtyard."

She looked around at the faces looking back at her before turning to Caroline. "I'll be right back."

"I'll be here," Caroline replied.

Morag ran for the stairs, going down them two at a time. Eddard was standing over by the well, his arms folded. He stood up straight when he saw her, taking a step in her direction. "I didnae ken if you'd gone," he said.

"I thought you might have left without saying goodbye," she replied.

"Are you not going back to your time?"

"This is my time," she said with a laugh. "I never realized but I am their daughter. I went to the future when I was little but now I'm back and I'm staying. If you'll have me."

He didn't smile. "I only brought you here so I could get into the treasury and get my money back."

"That's not true," she said with a shake of her head. "You're more than that. You wanted to get rid of Ronald so the clan would be free."

"Aye, well, maybe you're right."

"And what do you want now that's done?"

"The one thing neither your parents nor the King could give me."

"And what's that?"

"Someone who's infuriating and feisty and funny and beautiful and smarter than any woman I ken. A woman who doesnae need a man tae run her life but can run her own just fine."

"What if I want a man to run my life with me?"

"There are lots out there to choose from."

"What if the one I want is standing in front of me right now and all I want is for him to take me in his arms and kiss me?"

"Then I better do this." He threw his arms around her and planted a kiss on her lips.

It was a kiss like no other. Last time their lips touched she was filled with doubt and confusion as to his motives but this time it was very different.

The feel of him against her as the embrace deepened sent shivers through her. She barely heard the cheering coming from the keep.

Eddard heard, reluctantly moving his face away to look up. High above them the Laird and Lady had stepped out onto their balcony, Caroline alongside them. They were cheering and applauding.

Others stopped to look as the Laird called down. "You see before you the two people that saved this clan. Darkness swept over us like a blanket of evil but it has gone forever thanks to Eddard and our daughter who is returned to us after too long away.

"Tonight we feast in celebration of the return of Morag and to praise her companion, Eddard MacGregor, my new steward."

Chapter Fifteen

I t had been a long time since anyone had heard noise coming from the dungeon. The steward was still down there awaiting trial but his vitriolic curses and threats faded into silence as the days went by.

Life in the castle slowly returned to normal. Philip was on his way back from the monastery. Training sessions began to find new guards, urgent work as without them, the castle was undefended. The place often rang with the noise of swords hitting shields.

The enormous sword master, Garett, had his work cut out with some of the recruits. Many of the staff saw learning to fight as a chance to move up in the world. Garrett took them all on, though that led to shortages in the kitchen and the nearby farms.

Cam spent day after day in the great hall, Eddard by his side, along with the few other advisors they had been able to find. Many had died in exile, others refused to return, fearing that the clan was doomed. Enough made the journey back to make it possible to start again.

Dealing with the financial situation was the biggest headache. They could train all the guards they wanted. They could advertise for replacement staff from the peasants. The issue was finding the money to pay them.

"The clan's running on empty," Eddard said, running his eyes down to the bottom of the parchment laid out before him. "It cannae go on like this. You must stop paying them."

Cam shook his head. "I cannae do that. They would starve."

"We could feed them."

"There is little enough grain in the stores and no dried meat at all. It wouldnae last a month. They must have coin to buy from the markets. You're my steward. What do I need to do to resolve this?"

"Persuade the King to give you a little relief on the back taxes?"

"I can try but I doubt he'll listen. He has a war to fund."

"Aye and your clan saved the money that went to paying for it."

Cam leaned back in his chair. "We have been at this long enough. Clear the tables and prepare for his arrival."

The King was due that afternoon. The messenger had arrived the previous day with the missive day. There was no reason given for the visit which gave rise to speculation all over the castle.

Eddard rose and nodded to the Laird before withdrawing. If he was lucky he would be able to catch Morag on her way back to the castle. He left his scrolls in the muniments room before making his way outside to the courtyard.

There was a bite to the air. Summer was over and winter was coming, though slowly. He made his way out the gate, greeting the guards as he went. Outside people were making their way back and forth, coopers, blacksmiths, traders, all of them busy with getting the clan back on its feet.

It would take a long time. Ronald had years to

bleed the place dry. It would take more than a few weeks to fix things.

He put the thoughts out of his head. It was too nice an afternoon to think about the past. The wind was light, bearing the last of the summer warmth with good grace. The leaves on the trees were turning golden, the mountain tops dusted with the first of the snow.

It was almost possible to stop thinking about the upcoming winter, how hard it would be with no money for extra food. The farmers were doing their best to maximize their crops but there would be a lot of hungry people before the year was out.

Turning off the main track, he descended along the slope of a hillside toward the loch at the bottom. He saw her long before she saw him.

It had become a tradition of theirs. While he dealt with the Laird and the clan, she would swim. He could see her head bobbing as she made her way through the water. Caroline was beside her, the two of them talking as they swam.

The girl had blossomed since she'd first arrived, taking to life in the clan as if she'd always been one of the family. The same could be said of Morag.

Her memory had almost completely returned.

She would be able to give evidence in Ronald's trial. He would have to explain not only why he spent all the clan's money but also why he sent a little girl away from her parents for the entirety of her childhood.

He stopped at the edge of the loch and waited for them to emerge. It was hard not to smile at the peace he felt in his heart. It had been so long since he'd felt this way. All the time during his exile on Kirrin Island he had dreamed of being back home. He never really thought he had a chance.

She was the reason why. It was because of her that he was part of the clan. Not just part of it, steward to the Laird. When he thought of that his smile broadened. The impossible had come true thanks to her.

She saw him and waved, making her way through the water while Caroline continued swimming in lazy circles.

"Hello," she said, climbing out and accepting the towelling cloth he held out for her. "This is a pleasant surprise. What brings you down here?"

"The King is due soon. This might be our last bit for time together for a while."

"That bad, huh?"

He sat down on the grass, tossing a stone out into the water. It vanished from sight, ripples spreading slowly outward as she joined him. A moment later her hand was in his.

"I'm not sure if we're going to be able to solve this. The taxes would be a lot for a clan in good health and we're already struggling to get back on our feet. I dinnae ken what we're supposed to do."

"You'll think of something."

Caroline splashed over and climbed out, smiling at both of them. "Are we going up to get ready for the King coming?"

"I suppose we should," Eddard replied, getting to his feet.

"Don't worry," Morag said, squeezing his shoulder. "If the universe could bring us together, it can help you with this."

"I hope so."

They walked together, Eddard thinking what a strange family they had become. He and Morag were a couple for all intents and purposes. They were not wed but he intended to resolve that fairly shortly.

The clan had accepted Caroline as their daughter without asking any questions. He liked it that way. What was he supposed to tell anyone who asked?

Dinnae worry, she's from the future but you get used to her. They might not have burned witches for a few decades but old traditions died hard sometimes.

To his surprise the King was there when they returned to the castle. Outside his retinue were still making their way through the gate. "What's going on?" Morag asked.

"He must have got here early," Eddard replied. "Come on, we'll go in through the sally port."

He took them around the side of the walls to the tiny doorway in the far north corner, hidden behind two huge oak tree trunks. They squeezed inside, Eddard warning the guard in the corridor that it was him. The guard relaxed at once. "I almost had my sword in you. Why are you coming in this way?"

"Have you seen the main gate?"

"Not from in here."

Eddard headed down the corridor, calling back over his shoulder. "The King's arrived."

The King was nowhere to be seen, his horse being led to the stable. Deep in conversation with the Laird, a man with a crown upon his head paid no attention to the arrival of Eddard. "You," Eddard said as the man turned around. "You're not the King. You're…"

"Forbes MacCallister is my traveling name," the man replied, holding out a hand toward him. "William the rest of the time. And I ken your name of course."

"Your Majesty," Eddard said, inclining his head. Beside him Morag and Caroline curtseyed. "I had no idea."

"Which is the point of having a traveling name. Stand up, no man who saves a clan and the King's taxes in one day bows to anyone. And you must be Morag." He turned to kiss her hand. "I have heard much of the woman who tamed this man's heart and who is this child?"

"Caroline, your Majesty. Our daughter."

"Good day, Caroline. Now can we get inside and get some drinks in us? It has been a long hard ride."

Once they were in the great hall, it seemed as if the stores were not empty. Eddard looked at the food being served to the King and his retinue. He made a quick calculation. This one meal would use up a week's ration for the clan. He hoped it was worth it.

"I ken what you're thinking," Eddard whispered in Cam's ear. "We must make a good impression if we are to ask him to reduce our taxes."

The Laird began talking to the King about taxes. Eddard could just hear what was being said over the noise of the meal. "If you could just lower them a little, I would be most grateful, your Majesty."

"Later," William replied, waving him into silence. "I have something to say first."

He drained his tankard and stood up, thumping the table for silence. "I wish it to be known that Clan MacGregor is forevermore a noble clan."

A cheer went up from the MacGregors. The King waited for it to die down before continuing. "This man is responsible for saving the Royal coffers enough to fund this war against the English.

"With God on our side our nation will remain free and for that Eddard MacGregor has my personal thanks. As a token of our appreciation, I make this decree. No taxes for the next fifty years."

The roar that went up was deafening. The Laird beamed and Eddard smiled too, not because of what the King had said, but because when he said it, Morag's hand slipped into his underneath the table.

"Told you," she whispered in his ear, kissing him on the cheek a moment later.

"Eddard, will you stand?" the King asked.

Eddard did so, feeling the eyes of the room upon him.

"I thank you for what you did for me, for the clan, and for the Highlands."

The King bent a knee and a whisper went around the room. The King never bent a knee. It was unheard of.

Eddard nodded in response as the King sat and the meal resumed. He thumped his tankard on the table and the noise died down once more. "While I am standing, there is something I want to say."

He turned to face Morag. "The King of Scotland bends the knee to me but I bend my knee to you." He did so, pulling a small velvet bag from his pocket. "Morag MacGregor, I love you. Will you do me the honor of being my bride?"

She looked shocked, taking the ring from the bag and examining it as if it might disappear in a puff of smoke. "You're not serious?"

"Is that a yes?" the King shouted across.

"Yes!" she yelled, throwing her arms around Eddard and kissing him over and over. "Of course, yes. Yes with all my heart and soul."

Another cheer, the loudest noise coming from the King.

The meal went on around them once more but Eddard and Morag paid it no heed. They only had eyes for each other.

Epilogue

T he monk was standing on top of a barrel, the only way he could make sure everyone could see him. The clouds had been dark for days before the wedding but that morning they had parted.

"It is as if God himself wishes to observe and bless this union," he said when he arrived at the castle a little after ten.

Morag didn't hear her brother's kind words. She was too busy trying to keep calm. Behind her Caroline was helping with preparing her hair. The tradition was for it to be wrapped up and hidden away for the wedding but it was resisting all attempts.

Many a muttered word was said while her

unruly tresses were crammed into the coif, the barbette slipping from under her chin for what felt like the hundredth time. "It will go in," Caroline said. "Just keep still."

Morag did her best but it wasn't easy. At last she was given permission to stand up. She looked into the polished glass that served as a mirror. The reflection was hazy and indistinct but she could tell her hair was out of sight. "Do I look okay?" she asked.

"You look perfect," Rachel said from the doorway. "You remind me of me on my wedding day."

"Did you need to pee every eight minutes as well?"

"That's just nerves. You'll be fine."

By noon the last of the preparations were done. Morag made her way out into the courtyard. Fresh rushes had been laid down to protect her dress.

The gathered members of the clan stood aside to let her pass through them. All work had halted. Only the guards remained at their posts. Everyone else was there to watch the ceremony.

Caroline held her left hand, Rachel her right. They stopped halfway across the courtyard. "Hold," Cam shouted, a second after his cue. He marched over. "I demand to ken where my daughter is going in such finery."

"To be wed," Rachel replied, reciting the lines they'd rehearsed every day for a month. "She is to be wed to a good man and any who wish to protest have had three weeks to do so."

"Then I shall take her henceforth," Cam said, falling into step beside Morag, taking his wife's place. "As Laird of the clan, it is my duty."

They walked slowly the rest of the way, passing out of the gate and toward the chapel that lay a little way to the south. Abbot James was there, watching Philip climb onto a barrel. In front of him, Eddard stood resplendent in a new baldric, the colors of the tartan as bright as they would ever be.

The churchyard was filled to bursting with people, the sun shining down upon them. The chill wind that had filled the valley for the last few days was gone.

The last of the leaves on the trees fell still. Even the crows seemed to have settled into silence on the tops of the castle towers.

The monk held his hands up to the air, craning his neck back so far Jessica thought he might fall from his perch. Morag looked up at her baby brother, smiling as he nodded briefly her way before beginning his prayer.

It was lovely to see him home again. They had talked much since his return, her chance to bond with a sibling she never even knew she had. There he was, about to wed her to the man she loved. She felt so happy she thought she might burst.

"Oh Lord who is master of us all. We pray you will send your blessing to this couple who come together before us on this day to be bonded together for the rest of their lives in holy matrimony. Amen."

He turned to Eddard first. "You, Eddard MacGregor, of Clan MacGregor, agree before all gathered here that you shall take this woman to be your wife for the rest of your life, through strife and plenty, until death take you from this place?"

"Aye," Eddard replied, placing a hand over Morag's.

"And you, Morag MacGregor, of Clan MacGregor, agree before all gathered here that you shall take this man as your husband for the rest of your life, through strife and plenty, exile or welcome, darkness or light, until death take you from this place."

"Aye," Morag said as Eddard's slipped the ring onto her finger. "I do."

"Then we shall enter the church and Mass will be said over your first minutes as husband and wife."

After the service in the church was ended, the crowd headed for the great hall. The feast to be served would become a legend in MacGregor circles.

Since the King had decreed the clan would pay no taxes for fifty years, funds had become available that had previously been earmarked for the royal coffers.

Grain filled the stores, animals had been bought from other clans, the risk of a hungry winter had vanished. Not only that but rebuilding had begun on the crumbling battlements.

By the time the frost began, the castle would be well on the way to recovery, as if the steward had never laid his greedy hands on its treasury.

Morag sat at the high table with her husband on her left. To her right was Caroline and beside her Abbot James who had traveled from Kirrin Island for the occasion. Further on Cam sat with his wife.

Brother Philip had arrived back from the monastery in time to conduct the ceremony, Abbot

James gladly stepping aside to let him take over. Next to Philip was Angela who was knitting rather than eating as if she were at home by the fireside.

Morag looked at the clan, all of them eating, drinking, talking, laughing. It felt strange to think that it hadn't been long since she'd not known any of these people existed.

She thought back to the time before the key came in the mail. These people were all just ghosts from the ancient past then. Now they were living, breathing, human beings and she loved them all.

She tuned back into the conversation going on around her when she heard Ronald's name mentioned. That was one person she didn't love. She did feel sorry for him though.

He still languished in the dungeon. The King had been in no rush to conduct the trial. The war took precedence. Local justice would have to wait.

"I have spoken to the King and he approves if you do."

Cam frowned, standing up and walking over, tapping Eddard on the shoulder. "What do you think?"

"He told me this morning. I think it is a decision for the Laird to make."

"What's this about?" Morag asked.

"Not something that need disturb our wedding day," Eddard replied.

"You can't start a conversation and not finish it. What does the King approve of?"

"Abbot James has offered to take Ronald to the abbey prison. The King approves him being given a choice between remaining in the dungeon or becoming a novice monk."

"What if he becomes a monk and then escapes?" Philip asked.

"That is unlikely," Eddard said. "He would need to climb the walls and wander the island without being seen and he is guarded night and day. It would take a demon to manage it. He may be wicked but he is flesh and blood."

"What do you think?" Cam asked Morag. "You are the reason we're even here discussing this. Whatever you say, we shall do."

"I say let the abbot take him. He does no one any good rotting under the castle and we have no idea when the King may return to try him."

"So be it," Cam said, clapping his hands together.

"May we return to the wedding feast?" Rachel asked, beckoning her husband over. "If you're finished talking business, of course."

"Apologies, my dear," Cam said, going back to his seat.

Dancing began shortly afterward, the minstrels up in the gallery coming to life as the last of the food was finished. Morag danced with her husband, with her brother, with her father. She danced until her feet were sore and her head spun.

Long after the sun had set, she stopped, walking out with Eddard and Abbot James into the corridor beyond the great hall. They made their way up to the bedchamber, the door festooned with bouquets of heather. There they stopped.

"May this room be as blessed as your union," Abbot James said, genuflecting before them . "Amen."

He turned and walked away, leaving the two of them to make their way inside. "My wife," Eddard said, taking the armchair. "How does it feel?"

"Tiring," she replied, flopping back onto the bed. "I'm exhausted." She pulled the coif from her head, allowing her hair to fall free. "That's better. What? You're looking at me funny."

"Because of you the clan is saved," he said. "I'm still trying to work out how I got so lucky."

"Lucky?"

"To meet you. Because of you we found out

about the steward's plans, we saved the King's finances and he stopped our taxes. The castle is being rebuilt, the stores are full. We even have enough to endow the abbey and bring the villages up to standard.

"I even persuaded Cam to set aside a fund to rebuild the cottages on Kirrin Island, a job long overdue. All because you decided to help me."

She shook her head. "All I wanted to do was get home."

"You still want to go?"

"I am home. This is my home."

"Are you sure?"

"I wouldn't have married you if I wasn't. Besides, I no longer have the key."

"Where is it?"

"I lost it."

"Where?"

"I think it's gone where my mom's has gone, to wherever it's needed most. It's done its job, bringing us together. Now are you going to sit there all night or are you going to come over here and kiss me?"

He did a lot more than just kiss her that night. With their door closed, they confirmed their marriage in the ancient way.

Downstairs the feast continued until the early

hours. The minstrels played long into the night, the sound echoing out of the keep and into the countryside beyond.

When Morag slept that night, she dreamed of Kirrin Island. She was standing on the shore. In the morning light, far in the distance, there was a twinkle in a stream as a figure dropped a key into the water. It made its way slowly along and then out into the loch.

Hundreds of years later, the key would be found and open another door to the past. The figure who dropped it would be long gone by then. But they would also be just around the corner, as they always were.

Morag slept on, no idea how she knew what would happen to the key. When she awoke the next morning she told herself it was just a dream. Then she turned and touched her new husband on the cheek.

He awoke at once and drew her into his arms. And then they began their first morning together as a married couple . It began in the way all future mornings would begin, with the softest of kisses shared in the golden light of the dawn.

The End

Want to know what happens next to Clan MacGregor?
Get a bonus epilogue for free when you sign up for my newsletter here.

Author's Note

This is the second story in the MacGregor Clan series.

The first book, The Key in the Loch, featured Cam and Rachel and was set around 1180.

The third book, The Key to Her Heart features the son of Eddard and Morag, and is mostly set in and around 1240.

The fourth work, The Key to Her Past stars Wallace and Natalie and is set in and around 1270.

MacGregor Castle and the surrounding terrain are fictional but I have tried to make it all as realistic as possible regarding the time period.

The fifth book in the series is due out around October 2019. Sign up to my newsletter here to be the first to find out more.